Sparks

To Mandy and Christi

ıe blue,

st

of Debbie

Sparks

s. j. adams

f|ux™
Woodbury, Minnesota

First Edition
First Printing, 2011

Book design by Bob Gaul
Cover design by Lisa Novak
Cover art © Glenn Gustafson

Flux, an imprint of Llewellyn Worldwide Ltd.

Library of Congress Cataloging-in-Publication Data
Adams, S. J.
  Sparks : the epic, completely true blue, (almost) holy quest of Debbie /
S. J. Adams.—1st ed.
    p. cm.
  Summary: A sixteen-year-old lesbian tries to get over a crush on her reli-
gious best friend by embarking on a "holy quest" with a couple of misfits
who have invented a wacky, made-up faith called the Church of Blue.
  ISBN 978-0-7387-2676-2 (alk. paper)
[1. Self-perception—Fiction. 2. Religion—Fiction. 3. Lesbians—Fiction.
4. Des Moines (Iowa)—Fiction. 5. Humorous stories.] I. Title.
  PZ7.A21765Sp 2011
  [Fic]—dc23

                                                          2011022913

                                Flux
                      Llewellyn Worldwide Ltd.
                        2143 Wooddale Drive
                      Woodbury, MN 55125-2989
                           www.fluxnow.com

                  Printed in the United States of America

Acknowledgments

Thanks to Ronni, of course, and to Jennifer Laughran, to Brian Farrey, and to everyone at Flux.

Also, thanks to Andrew Karre, Jessi Dunlap, Jonathan Spring, Amanda Walters, Hector Reyes, Willie Williams, Nadia Cornier, Jen Hathy, Jeff Jeske, Deborah Sacks, Amy Vincent, Julie Halpern, James Klise, James Kennedy, my family, the Smart Aleck staff, and the cast and crew of *Full House*.

I would be remiss if I didn't point out that my "Ragged Glory: Debbie Does Detention" playlist has been the heart and soul of this project from the beginning. So thanks to The Beach Boys, Kimya Dawson, The Hold Steady, Neko Case, The Mountain Goats, Pearl Jam, Neutral Milk Hotel, The Long Blondes, The Moldy Peaches, Counting Crows, Bob Dylan, The Ike Reilly Assassination, Miracle Legion, Polaris, Vixy and Tony, Seanan McGuire, Ben Folds, Regina Spektor, and Tom Waits.

✴ One ✴

My dad's a regular guy, and my mom's a total kook, so I guess I had a fifty percent chance of coming out normal. Leave it to me to screw it up.

When I was a kid, Mom was always saying things like, "You know, Debbie, a lot of girls find out they have psychic abilities when they hit puberty. Maybe you'll be one of them!" That was her idea of encouraging me to dream big. I think she was very disappointed when I started shaving my legs and didn't suddenly remember that I was a plowman in a former life or something.

I assume that it was all her fault when Dad moved to Minneapolis to live with another woman when I was twelve. I didn't exactly blame him. It was probably either that or get dragged to another "couples retreat" where he'd have to dance around naked with middle-aged strangers and eat figs.

And I'm one hundred percent certain that it's her fault that I always feel like people can read my mind. I work really, really hard not to think about sex or having to pee or anything embarrassing like that when I'm in class, because I just can't shake the feeling that someone in there—maybe everyone—will be able to tell what I'm thinking about just by looking at me. I know that they can't, really, but I always *feel* like they can.

When I'm in public and something personal comes into my head, I count to twenty-five over and over and just focus on the numbers, hoping that even if it doesn't get anything all the way out of my head, maybe I can at least jam the signal for any mind readers who happen to be nearby.

And that's what I was doing on the cloudy Friday morning before my junior year spring break as I rode to school in Lisa Ashby's car.

"When he holds my hand, he does this thing where he rubs one of his fingers between my thumb and index finger," Lisa said. "Like, back and forth, back and forth. Its a-mazing."

1, 2, 3, 4...

Lisa, my best friend of all time, was driving me to school and talking about her new boyfriend, Norman Hastings, who's probably the most boring human being on the planet. I didn't want her reading my mind and knowing that I thought she was making a huge mistake.

"My next project is going to be to get him to stop dressing like he's going fishing for trout," she said.

"Fishing for trout?"

"Yeah. When he's not in school, he dresses like he fell out of an Eddie Bauer catalog or something. If you saw him on the street, you'd say, 'Now, there goes a guy who's going fishing for trout!'"

I chuckled in spite of myself. Lisa was the funniest person I'd ever known. No matter how upset I was, she could always make me laugh.

To me, Norman looked like ... well, he just looked like a *Norman*. He looked like he had taken a picture of a doctor from an old pamphlet about venereal disease to the barber and said, "Make me look like this!" And he was one of about six people in school who took the option of wearing a shirt and tie rather than the normal uniform (a plain shirt in blue or white, the school colors, with iron-on lettering optional if you insist on expressing yourself).

"Oh, and hey," Lisa said. "I probably can't give you a ride home today. I've got some stuff going on with Jennifer Pratt."

"That's okay," I said. "I can walk. It probably won't start raining until late."

Lisa had turned the radio off right after they'd said that Omaha was expecting the biggest storm in five years, and we always get Nebraska's weather here in central Iowa a few hours later. There was still some blue sky above us, but dark clouds were already rolling in from the west.

"And I won't be able to watch TV tonight, obviously," Lisa went on.

"No problem," I said, as if it didn't matter.

But it did. It mattered a *lot*.

1, 2, 3, 4, 5, 6 ...

It's amazing how much it hurts to see your best friend hooking up with a loser.

And Lisa wasn't just my best friend, she was also pretty much my *only* friend. She and I had spent every Friday night since sixth grade in her bedroom watching cheesy old family sitcoms—the kind where every episode ends with someone getting a lecture with soft music in the background, followed by everyone hugging. *Full House*, mostly. We'd been through that whole series four times. It was our thing.

Honestly, I'd have preferred to be watching something more "adult," but Lisa and her family were really religious. They thought shows where people swear or have premarital sex were trashy, and I just went with the flow. I even went to ACTs (Active Christian Teens) with her, despite the fact that I was really sort of an atheist. Keeping my thoughts to myself at those meetings was stressful enough to give me migraines.

And now I'd been dumped. Cast aside. Left behind. My services as a friend were no longer needed. I'd been blown off for the last boy on the planet to be named Norman.

NORMAN!

As soon as we got out of the car, Norman and a couple of his friends from the FCA (Fellowship of Christian Athletes) started walking toward us.

"Here he comes," she almost sang.

She skipped away from me (yes, skipped) over to Norman and his boring FCA friends. I half expected her to break into song or something.

And here's the thing: I don't think anyone in Lisa's family would be against it if she and Norman got *engaged* by the end of high school. Getting a ring as a graduation gift next year was a distinct possibility for her.

Lisa was raised to believe that you're supposed to fall in love at sixteen, marry your high school sweetheart when you're nineteen or twenty, and be a mommy nine months later. I don't think her parents ever heard of a marriage they didn't think was a good idea (as long as it was between a man and a woman), and I think they were more disturbed by my parents' divorce than I was. It's almost like they had a marriage fetish. Probably a prayer fetish, too.

As soon as I thought of that, I had to push the image of Lisa breathing heavier and heavier while Norman prayed over her out of my brain. Out, out, out! She was still just a couple of feet away from me—prime thought-reading range.

I was going to need to find a new best friend. Fast.

I raced through the parking lot and into school as fast as I could, then ducked into the first bathroom I came to. Angela Mackenzie, another girl from ACTs who sat with us at lunch, was doing her makeup in the mirror. Next to her was an overweight girl with short blond hair that she'd done a pretty bad job of dying red and the kind of pointy glasses waitresses in movies always wear.

She nodded at me and I nodded back at her, then I turned to Angela. "Doing anything for spring break?" I asked.

She put her lipstick back in her purse and dug out an eyebrow pencil.

"Babysitting, mostly," she said. "Picking up an overnight gig in Urbandale tonight."

"I'm staying in town, too," I said. "Maybe we can hang out."

"Sure," she said. "I'll give you a call."

I doubted that she actually would. She was nice, but she was also one of those people who's friends with everyone in town, so she couldn't possibly have had much time for me.

Still, I knew that I needed to loosen up a little. Angela could help. She went to ACTs and all, but I knew she'd slept with a guy or two.

She was wearing a T-shirt that said *One Year, Three Months!* The time left until graduation, I think.

Cornersville Trace High School is the only school

in the Des Moines metro area that has a uniform policy, as far as I know. The whole thing of ironing words onto uniforms is new; the reason they started making us wear uniforms in the first place had less to do with stifling free expression than stopping kids from having to worry about name-brand clothes, but when a bunch of kids complained that it *did* stifle free expression, the school board compromised. Now you could iron words onto your shirt in plain block letters, as long as the words weren't obscene or about drugs or gangs.

Lisa's T-shirt that day read *Get High on Love!*

The heavyset girl beside Angela was wearing one that said *Tangled Up in Blue*, whatever that meant.

Mine was plain white.

"Can you believe Lisa is actually going out with that Norman guy?" I asked.

"Seriously," said Angela. "She could do better."

"Hastings?" asked the other girl. "Barf-o-rama."

"I don't know what Lisa even sees in him," I said as I leaned against the wall. "I mean, she's so funny, and he's so boring!"

"Security," said Angela. "His dad owns ones of those car lots on Merle Hay Road. He's totally loaded."

"That can't be it," I asked. "I mean, she's, like … perfect. She's cute, she's smart, she's funny. She's the kind of person everyone wants to be."

"So?" asked Angela.

"So, Norman is the kind of person everyone wants to punch."

"Oh, for sure," Angela agreed. "He's boring as hell, and he's a major assho…" She stopped herself mid-swear and said, "Jerk. Major jerk."

Lisa's reputation as a goody-goody had rubbed off on me. And why shouldn't it have? I'd practically willed it to.

"You can say the A-word in front of me," I said. "Lisa's the one who's weird about cursing. I've actually been thinking about staging an intervention to get her to just say 'ass' instead of 'tushy.'"

Angela chuckled. "Today, the A-word, tomorrow, the F-bomb!"

"Heh," said the other girl. "In a way, you and Norman are both building her up to a fuck."

Angela laughed. "Nice one, Emma."

It took me a second to get the joke. When I did, I turned my head and slumped into the wall. The cold, glossy paint was cold against my ear.

"And she probably doesn't even know it, if he is," I said. "She probably thinks that only guys who take auto shop actually want to have premarital sex."

"No one's *that* naïve," said Angela.

"She might be," I said. "She watches a whole lot of *Full House*, you know."

Angela chuckled. "Are you guys going to that ACTs picnic on Tuesday?"

"I don't think I'm going to go to freaking ACTs at all anymore."

I hadn't wanted to say "freaking," but the right word just didn't come out. Lisa and her family had sunk their claws too far into me.

"Gonna join Fellowship of Christian Athletes instead?"

"Hell no."

Angela seemed kind of amused at how upset I was. "What?" she asked. "You don't like Christian bowling?"

"Christian bowling?" asked Emma, the other girl. "What, do the pins rise again on the third frame?"

Angela snickered. I probably would have laughed, too, if I didn't feel like my guts were about to fall apart.

Then Emma turned away from the mirror and looked right at me. "You okay?" she asked.

"I'm just trying to figure out what the hell I'm going to do tonight. I'm so used to hanging out with Lisa on Fridays. And she's, like, ditching me. It's throwing my whole routine off."

"Creature of habit, huh?" said Angela.

"Totally."

Emma smiled, which bugged me. "You feel lost? Alone?" she asked.

I just shrugged. I'd seen Emma around, hanging out with this one guy, Tim Sanders, who I'd heard was gay, but I didn't know her well enough to want her advice or anything.

"I know something that might help," she said.

"If you say Jesus, I'll punch you in the face," I said.

She laughed, and just as she did, the first bell rang. I ran off toward my first class before she could say anything.

Lisa was lost in a world where a future with a guy named Norman who wore ties to high school was something to skip about. And I was left by myself. At sixteen, I was going to have to either face life as a total loner, tag along on Lisa and Norman's dates, or just, like, restart my whole adolescence.

I collapsed into my first-period desk, which was the most uncomfortable desk on the planet. The chair was attached to the desk and the cold metal of the legs rubbed against my knees no matter how I tried to position myself.

While everyone else talked about their spring break plans (which made them too busy to bother with reading my mind, I hoped), I repeated to myself that I was my own person, not just half of Lisa-and-Debbie. That I didn't need Lisa just to exist—I wasn't just her wacky friend and sidekick, like Kimmy Gibbler, D. J. Tanner's weird friend on *Full House*.

I repeated it, but I didn't totally believe it.

In an attempt to reassure myself, I made a list while I waited for class to start.

Reasons I'm Not Like a Full House Character (especially Kimmy Gibbler)

1. I sometimes say curse words you can't say on family TV (at least in private).

2. My feet don't smell so bad they could set off a smoke alarm, like Kimmy's.

3. ~~I'm failing science.~~ (Had to cross this out after I remembered the episode where D. J. gets an F for her paper on photosynthesis.)

4. I don't go around hugging people. Much.

5. I've never snuck out of school to get a rock star's autograph, or secretly arranged to study with boys, or helped anyone sneak into a movie theater.

6. I have never taken a trip to Vegas or Hawaii or Disney World.

7. I have never come down with amnesia and needed clips from previous episodes to jar my memory.

I crossed out numbers 5–7 because they were all ways the people on *Full House* had *more* exciting, daring lives than I did, which was just depressing.

It was starting to look like the only difference between me and a wacky sidekick was that I wasn't very wacky.

So just before the bell rang, I wrote down The Big One. In really tiny letters. The one I'd never written down anywhere, not even in my diary. The one I certainly hadn't said out loud or even thought about when anyone else was in the room with me.

8. I'm reasonably sure that the reason Kimmy hung out with D. J. was NOT because she'd had a stupid, hopeless crush on her for years.

So there, Gibbler. You can kiss my ass.

✳ Two ✳

I counted to twenty-five again and again and again as I folded that list into a tiny wad and put it in my backpack. I was too afraid to rip it up and put it in the trash, because if I did, I knew I'd spend weeks imagining that someone had gone through the trash and managed to put all the tiny pieces back together again.

It's not like I hadn't *known* it was a crush. I'd been through the whole internal struggle of realizing I liked girls years before. I'd even told my dad without any real drama. I hadn't told Mom yet, but only because I was afraid she'd sign me up for workshops where they'd tell me I was a bad lesbian if I didn't change my name to Willow and stop shaving my armpits.

But I didn't want to risk freaking Lisa out and

making her not want me hanging around her anymore, so I'd never told her. I could live with her not loving me back, but not with her pushing me away. I needed her, at least as a friend.

The teacher, Mrs. Malatesta, came into the room, carrying an armload of worksheets, a cup of coffee, and a stack of books.

"Good morning," she mumbled. "We have a lot to get done before spring break, so everybody sit down and shut up."

The sheer notion of getting anything done was insane. Everyone was already in spring break mode, mentally. I was lost in my own world, trying to get my mind off Lisa and onto something nasty, like popping zits, so that anyone who was reading my mind would get grossed out and stop.

Mrs. Malatesta put down her armload of papers and picked up an attendance sheet. She mostly just looked for people and then made a mark next to their name, until she got to mine.

"Debbie Woodlawn?" she said. "Debbie, are you here?"

"Here," I said.

She looked up. "Oh, there you are, Debbie," she said. "I didn't see you there."

Yeah. Her or anyone else.

I always tended to blend in with my surroundings, but that was just the way I wanted it right then. The fewer people there were paying attention to me, the fewer there were who might be reading my mind.

Fifty minutes later I was back in the hallway, wondering where I should be standing, where I should be looking, and what I should be saying.

Everyone had divided into their groups already. Cheerleaders were on one side of the hall. Punk rock kids were on another. There were a couple of emo kids near the bathroom, and the stoners were in a cluster by the drinking fountain.

Which of the groups in the hall would I have been in if I hadn't started being friends with Lisa back when I was eleven? What was I even *like* back when I was ten? I remembered being into horses and gossiping and Disney movies, but that seemed like it was a hundred years ago. Was that same person still even inside of me?

And what did it matter? I couldn't go back to acting like a ten-year-old.

But I knew that I was going to have to stop being The Girl Who Hangs Out with Lisa and start being myself. Whoever the hell that was.

The goth kids always looked about as depressed as I felt, so that was a possibility, but I didn't think they'd let me hang out with them. It's hard to get in with the goth crowd if you weren't, like, born a goth. If I tried to hang out with them after years of being The Girl Who Hangs Out with Lisa Ashby, they'd probably call me a poseur or something.

The cheerleaders on the other side of the hall probably wouldn't let me near them, either. One thing I've got to give them credit for is that at least they have a formalized processed for joining their group—they have try-outs. The only other groups I could think of that have a process like that are the theater kids, who have auditions, and gangsters, who I always heard make you kill someone for their shoes or something. The wannabes (the kind of gangsters we have around suburban Des Moines, at least on the West Side) probably really just make you steal a pack of gum from the Quick Trip or something, which I could probably pull off, but there's no way they'd be the group for me anyway.

I was about to duck into my next class early, just to get the hell out of the hall, when Emma, the overweight girl from the bathroom in the *Tangled Up in Blue* shirt, came up to me.

"Hey," she said.

"Hey," I said back.

"I wasn't going to tell you about Jesus," she said. "I have something else that might help you out."

"I can't afford drugs," I said.

She chuckled. "Not that, either. Another religion."

I started walking away, but she followed me.

"She's not just your friend, is she?" she asked.

I stopped dead in my tracks and turned toward her.

"What are you talking about?" I asked, praying to any

deity who might be listening that this wasn't proof that people could read my mind after all.

"Come on," she said. "No one gets this broken up or stops going to ACTs because their best friend is dating an asshole."

I felt myself going a bit short of breath.

"Whatever," I said.

"Hey, don't worry," she said. "It's nothing to be ashamed of. My religion doesn't have a problem with it."

I sighed. "Fine, I'll bite," I said. "What's your religion?"

"The Church of Blue," she said. "Bluedaism. It's the best religion ever."

"I'm not really in the market for a new religion," I said as I started to walk away again. "My mom's already tried them all."

"Not this one," she said. "Trust me. For five bucks, I'll tell you all about it and take you on a holy quest."

"You think I'm gonna give you five bucks to hear about a religion?"

"All the best religions cost money," she said. "People don't take things they get for free seriously. But it's totally tax deductible. Probably."

"I'll pass," I said.

"Just keep it in mind. Active Bluish Teens do way cooler stuff than bowling. We got George Washington's autograph last week."

I stared at her for a second. "You guys raise the dead?"

She chuckled. "Not *that* George Washington. The old

black guy named George Washington who lives out in Ankeny. It was part of a holy quest. I'll bet they don't do *that* in the FCA."

"I'll think it over and let you know," I said.

And I walked along to my next class.

I really wanted someone to hang out with that night, so I didn't want to burn any bridges, but Emma struck me as a real freak. And it disturbed me, in a way, to hear her talking about me liking Lisa right out loud, like it wasn't that big of a deal. Because it was. It was, like, the biggest deal ever.

In my next class, I sat next to a hairy guy named Nate Spoelstra. The fact that he wasn't attractive didn't stop him from coming on to anything with breasts—including me.

"Hey," said Nate when I sat down.

"Hey," I mumbled.

Nate scratched the back of his head for a second—he did a lot of scratching in any given day. A couple of stray hairs would fly off the back of his head each time, and sometimes they ended up on my desk. He shed enough hair in a day it's a wonder any was left, but somehow it just kept coming back. I wouldn't have thought this out loud at an ACTs event, but it seemed like Nate was proof we're related to apes. He looked like he hadn't quite evolved all the way.

Mr. Lombardo, the teacher, wandered in looking like he'd just climbed out of a coffin—he always had the pale, clammy look of a guy who's been dead for a day or two. He picked up the attendance sheet to take the roll, and one of the Outdoor Kids (the ones who always hang around by the window and run to the front door just to be outside between classes) raised her hand.

"Can we have class outside today?" she asked, without waiting to be called on.

"No," said Mr. Lombardo.

"Come on!" the girl pleaded. "We're all suffocating in here! Right, guys?"

"Eighty percent chance of thundershowers today," said Mr. Lombardo. "And a chance of tornados. Last thing I need to do is bring the school's insurance rates up."

It wasn't going to start raining for several hours, but the girl should have known it was hopeless. You could just look at Mr. Lombardo's skin and tell he didn't like going outside much.

The Outdoor Kids were a group I hadn't thought about joining. But I didn't feel like the sun gave me energy, like they always said it did for them. I think that only works for plants.

I took better notes in Chemistry that day than ever before in my freaking life. I wrote down every damn thing Mr. Lombardo said, even the stuff about his dogs that was totally off topic. It gave me something to think about besides Lisa.

Still, she kept creeping back into my brain—her smile, her hair, the way she never seemed unhappy for even a second. Every joke she'd ever told me.

Every time I noticed Mr. Lombardo looking like a corpse, which was about every thirty seconds, I remembered all the stuff Lisa had said about him when she'd had him last semester.

"He looks like he's not even human," she'd said. "Maybe some other teacher built him as a science project and forgot to add pigment to his skin!"

Ever since she said that, I had a hard time looking at Mr. Lombardo without laughing. That might have been why I was failing his class.

Halfway through class, Hairy Nate passed me a note.

Doing anything for spring break? it said.

I wrote *maybe* below it and passed it to him.

Gonna party, then? he wrote back.

I just shrugged, and he sent me another note.

I get off work at the Burger Box at 7. Call me. 266-1727.

I put the note in my pocket and gave him a "we'll see" shrug.

It wasn't the first time I'd ever had a guy try to hook up with me (I'm not gorgeous or anything, but I'm pretty cute, if I do say so myself—cute face, golden-blond hair that shines no matter what I put in it, decent body), but this would have been the first time I ever even thought about saying "yes." I was getting desperate. *Anything* sounded better than sitting at home, alone, while Lisa was out with Norman.

I spent a minute trying to talk myself into liking Nate. I wasn't totally sure if I was gay or bi or what yet, officially, so I supposed I could try dating a guy. Sure, he was hairy, but wasn't it kind of mean of me to think he wasn't worth hanging out with just because he seemed kind of gross? You can't control how fast your hair grows, right?

But then I decided that it wasn't the hair so much as the grease that made him gross. And the fact that, right after Mr. Lombardo stopped talking and let us just work on our chemical-reaction worksheets, Nate started picking his nose and talking about wrestling with the guy who sat on the other side of him. And then they started talking about getting "fucked up."

I could picture a night with Hairy Nate—I would sit around trying to keep him from doing anything stupid while he drank, smoked, shouted at a wrestling match on TV, and shed all over the couch until it was time for us to do it.

And for just a moment, I went back to thinking of Lisa as an angel who had kept me on the straight and narrow path and saved me from guys who reminded me of skinny gorillas. But I knew I couldn't let myself think of Lisa like that. Not anymore. I was going to have to start saving myself.

Even if, by some miracle, she dumped Norman and went back to hanging out with me, I couldn't go on like this. Living in her perfect version of the world was probably giving me so many ulcers that my stomach would look like a slimy hunk of Swiss cheese by the time I was thirty.

I had spent five years pretending to be her girlfriend, never stopping to think that it was all going to have to come to an end eventually. But now it had. Things would never be the way they were again. All I could do was try to take control of the way things had changed.

The whole idea of, like, declaring myself to Lisa, or whatever you call it, scared the heck out of me, but the only other option if I wanted to be with her was to murder Norman Hastings, then be there to comfort her while the cops looked for his head.

It may not have been practical, but at least it was an idea that never would have occurred to anyone on *Full House*. And it gave me something relatively safe to think of through the next couple of periods, until it was time for lunch.

Which would be at my usual table. With Lisa.

✳ Three ✳

After obsessing over her all morning, it was weird seeing Lisa sitting there at the table, smiling that super-cute smile of hers, oblivious to the fact that she'd been haunting me all day.

But lunch was clearly not the best time to tell her how I felt. There were too many other people around. Even if she secretly *did* love me back, she'd probably have to act like she didn't in case anyone who might tell her parents overheard. My best chance would be getting her alone later.

I was just going to have to get through lunch, and maybe drop some hints to lay the groundwork for later.

"Hi, Debbie," Lisa said cheerfully as I sat down. I'd

felt like I was sloshing through a dirty gutter all morning, and she seemed like she'd been floating on a cloud.

"Hey," I said, as I tried to smile and look cute.

"Get through Chemistry okay?" she asked. She always remembered when I had trouble in a class. She was thoughtful like that.

"Not really," I said. "I think I'm failing."

"Oh no," said Lisa. "Don't worry. Look at the window. See those clouds?"

Out the window, I could see the clouds getting darker and closer, like they were peering through the window at us. It almost looked like nighttime. Maybe I'd get lucky and a tornado would blow me to Oz.

"So it's gonna rain tonight," I said. "What's that got to do with anything?"

"Maybe whoever built Mr. Lombardo made him water soluble," she said. "As soon as he gets wet, he'll just, like, wash away."

She laughed, and I laughed, too. Even when her jokes weren't *that* funny, her laugh was so infectious that I always cracked up whenever she did.

This was part of why I loved her. If you had a problem, she'd make you feel better. She'd bend over backward to do it, if she had to. She could make a joke out of anything.

And then she reached out and squeezed my hand. Just, like, to reassure me, not out of affection, but I smiled. It was one of those stupid, teasing moments that gave me hope that maybe she had a secret crush on me, too. I lived for those moments. But they really just made it all worse in the long run.

The more she hung out with Norman, the less she'd be holding my hand or touching me. Thinking of that made it suddenly seem difficult to breathe, and trying to smile and look cute got harder and harder.

Angela came in and sat down beside Lisa and across from me.

"Hey guys," she said. "How's Norman?"

Lisa let go of my hand to hold it to her chest. "It's like a dream," she said.

Angela grinned. "I've had those kind of dreams."

"Me too," said Lisa. "Only now it's coming true!"

Angela grinned at me sneakily, like she was expecting me to share in the joke that Lisa hadn't even realized she was talking about sex dreams, but I just felt worse. I pulled my lunch out of my backpack and fished out my sandwich.

"What are you red hot lovers doing tonight?" Angela asked.

"We *were* going to go miniature golfing and then hit a late movie," said Lisa. "But since it's going to rain, we'll probably just go to an earlier movie *and* a late one."

"Which ones?"

"Who cares?"

Angela snickered. "Not planning to watch them, huh?"

And Lisa clapped her hands like a five-year-old at a birthday party.

"So," asked Angela, "has he...you know?"

"Kissed me?" Lisa grinned.

Angela nodded.

Lisa smiled so big she'd probably be sore in the morning. "Like, a million times!"

1, 2, 3, 4, 5...

"Gone any further?" asked Angela.

Lisa just smiled. "We've sort of taken a lead off first, but I haven't let him go to second yet."

Yet.

My innards did another quarter turn inside of me.

"Well, over the course of two movies, I imagine you'll get around to something," said Angela.

"I'm not sure two movies will be enough," Lisa giggled.

I guess I'd wanted to believe that Lisa was actually blinded into thinking that normal people didn't really have premarital sex by all those *Full House* episodes where Becky comes over to see Uncle Jesse in the morning— she's never still there from the night before until after the wedding episode. Actually, if you read between the lines, I think the writers made it pretty clear that they were doing it *way* earlier than that, but they had to keep it on the down-low to fool the kids. I had thought—hoped— they'd fooled Lisa, too.

What was she thinking, acting like this?

The teenagers on the shows she watched never went to second. Sometimes they had *friends* who did, but they always ended up regretting it. Sometimes they even got pregnant. Or AIDS, if it was one of those "very special episodes."

My chest started tightening and my vision got blurry. I felt like every cloud outside had rolled in through the window and just, like, enveloped me. Pinned me down. It was the kind of feeling I always get right before a panic attack.

I started thinking "I love you" right out loud, loud enough that Lisa should have been able to read my thoughts even if she wasn't trying to. Loud enough that the whole school should have turned their heads and looked over to see what the ruckus was all about.

But they didn't notice, and neither did she.

Then, of course, things got worse.

"Anyway," Lisa said to me, "now that I've found true love, we need to find someone for you! We can double date!"

"Yeah," I said. "I totally need a boyfriend."

"I can see if Norman has any single friends," she said, like Norman would have any friends that I would even like.

I went back to staring at my sandwich, so I had no idea that Norman was walking up to the table until I heard him say, "Hey, babe."

Who in the hell actually calls girls "babe"?

I mean, people talk like that all the time on *Full House,* but that was years ago. And I'll bet people didn't even *really* talk like that back then.

Norman was wearing the shirt-and-tie combo he

always wore—he said it was "the Christian way to dress," which I'm pretty sure was a load of crap. As far as I could tell from the videos we watched in ACTs, the "Christian way to dress" is robes and sandals.

I mean, what about that point on the end of the tie? Didn't Norman know what it was pointing *at*?

Norman motioned for Angela to scooch over and sat down in her place, next to Lisa. I was sitting on the other side of the table, pretending not to notice that my foot was bumping against hers.

"I was just telling Debbie we need to find someone for her, so we can double date," said Lisa.

"There are a some cool guys in the FCA," said Norman. "Do you know Aaron Riley?"

Aaron wore shirts and ties to school, too. But not because of religious reasons. I'm pretty sure he thought that if it ever came out that he'd ever worn something other than business attire, he'd be barred from working at a Fortune 500 company.

I would rather date Hairy Nate.

I didn't say this out loud, of course. I just nodded while I counted to twenty-five in my head.

"Riley's a good guy," said Norman. "He's single now, too, since he dumped Gia Van Atta. You know she's slept with four guys?"

"Really?" asked Lisa.

"So I hear," said Norman. "That's why he dumped

her. And I'll bet that means she's given a you-know-what to at least, like, ten."

"A you-know-what?" asked Angela. "Why don't you just say it, if we all know what it is?"

Norman gave her a weird look.

"Are you sure that's even true?" Angela went on. I could tell she was kind of offended, since she'd probably given a you-know-what to a few guys herself.

"I have it on good authority," said Norman, confidently.

This was why I couldn't possibly talk to Lisa about how I felt at lunch. I couldn't even hint at it now that Norman was there. If Norman had any notion that *either* of us liked girls, he'd tell e*veryone* and people would be organizing "prayer warrior" meetings for us.

"Ew," said Lisa. "I don't think it's really that big of a sin to do, like, more than kissing before you're married, but you should at least only do it with one person that you really love!"

Then I saw Norman sneakily move his arm around Lisa's waist and pull her in closer. She put her head onto his shoulder.

With every fiber of my being, I wanted to jump up out of my seat, stand on the table, summon a bunch of spooky flashing lights, and shout "get your hands off her!" in a voice that would shake the windows and rattle the walls. I felt like the two of them had just reached into my chest, grabbed my heart, and squeezed it really, really hard, like it was a grapefruit and they were trying to make juice or whatever. My eyes went blurry and my stomach started to hurt so badly I thought it was trying to break out through my belly button.

When I saw Norman leaning over to kiss Lisa on the cheek, I finally snapped.

I picked up my brown paper lunch bag, swung it over my head, and slammed it onto the table. Hard. So hard that the bag ripped open and the container of yogurt inside of it cracked. Some pink yogurt goop spurted out and sprayed the table. Some of it bounced back onto my top, but it managed to miss Norman's stupid shirt entirely.

"God damn it!" I shouted.

I didn't wait around to see Lisa's reaction. I got up, grabbed my purse, and stomped away from the table toward the hall.

As I stormed through the cafeteria, I saw Emma, the weird girl, sitting at a table with Tim, the gay guy. She tried to get my attention as I walked past, but I didn't even slow down. I marched clear out of the cafeteria, past the drama hall and down another hall, then into the last bathroom before the side exit to the parking lot.

Inside of it, I slumped against the wall, intending to just stay there, but when I looked up I realized that I'd walked into the boys' restroom. There were urinals. No boys peeing, thank God, but urinals.

"God damn!" I shouted again, louder this time. I smacked my hand hard against the floor and felt the cold sting of the ceramic tiles against my palm. Then I smacked it again.

What else could possibly go wrong?

All those years of watching cheesy sitcoms should have taught me never, ever to think that.

I got out of the boys' bathroom and went into the girls' room next door, kicked open the door to one of the stalls, and sat down on the toilet. As soon as I sat down, the crying started.

I don't think I'd cried like that, with all of the noises and wailing and stuff, since I was about four or five. If I'd ever wondered about it, I would have thought that I couldn't do it anymore. But it's like riding a bike, I guess. You get so good at bawling when you're a baby that your body never really forgets how to do it.

That boring asshole in the tie had stolen my imaginary girlfriend.

I'd wasted my entire youth—from age eleven to age sixteen-and-a-half, anyway—for Lisa. Instead of going to parties or whatever, I'd spent my high school years watching cheesy old TV shows and trying to live like I was a character in one of them.

I never even really expected her to kiss me, or sleep with me, or touch me, or any of that stuff. I was happy just to be with her. It was something. It was enough.

Only now it was nothing.

I had pretended to be religious for her. I had acted as if a little kid saying, "You got it, dude" or a second grader saying, "How rude" was the height of comedy. Even when I was on my own, I had avoided watching TV shows or listening to music that I didn't think she'd approve of. I had never argued with her when she said people I kind of liked having around were probably going to hell.

I'd even played along in a big ceremony where the whole group from ACTs put on these sterling silver rings that were supposed to symbolize a vow of chastity. I kept the ring on even though it was the wrong size for me.

Now I took it off and dropped it into the toilet.

Hell, part of why I'd stayed in Iowa with my crazy mom instead of going to Minneapolis with Dad was to stay close to Lisa. I liked it in Minneapolis. I liked his new wife, Reine, who I guessed was technically my stepmom.

Maybe I could go live there, where no one knew a thing about me, and be a totally different person.

I counted to twenty-five a whole bunch of times, but it didn't change a thing. It never really did.

A minute later, someone walked into the restroom.

"Debbie?" a voice called out. "Are you in here?"

It was Angela.

I didn't say anything, but I sniffed really loud.

She walked up to the stall door. "Are you decent," she asked, "or are you peeing?"

"Decent," I muttered. "Come on in."

She opened up the stall door. There was no point in

trying to cover up the fact that I'd been crying. My face was probably as red as a monkey's butt.

"Oh my God," she said. "Are you okay?"

I just stared at her. I wasn't going to dignify that with a response.

"Jesus," she said. "Are you *that* upset about Norman?"

I shook my head.

"Don't worry," she said. "You won't be single forever. I'm sure I can find you someone better than Aaron Riley. That guy's a douche."

"It's not like that!" I snapped.

She took a step backward. I'd never snapped at her like that.

"Lisa wanted to come have a talk with you herself," she said.

I snorted. "She'd give me a speech about how we'll always be friends, no matter what happens, and then we'd hug. There'd be slow saxophone music in the background and the crowd would go 'Awww' and everything would be all better."

Angela laughed. "Yeah, that's probably exactly what she had in mind. What would you rather she do, though? You can't just expect her to wait until you find a boyfriend before she starts seeing anyone herself."

"I told you. It's *not like that*," I said. I stared straight down at the toilet to keep from looking her in the eyes.

Maybe she read my thoughts, or maybe she just put the pieces together.

"Oh my freaking God," said Angela. "You…"

I just nodded.

Angela didn't say anything for a second, so I spoke instead.

"If you tell her, I'll kill you. I'll kill you so hard your parents will die, too. And your children's children's children."

For a second, neither of us said anything, but I got the impression that she was trying hard not to laugh.

"Damn it," I said, "will you stop staring at me? Haven't you ever seen a lesbian having a panic attack on a toilet before?"

She allowed herself to giggle a bit. "Not one with that much yogurt on her shirt."

I just looked down. I could still see the chastity ring at the bottom of the toilet bowl.

"Sorry, Deb," she said. "I didn't realize … well, you know Lisa likes *guys*, right?"

I nodded. I guess I was hoping she didn't, really, and was just pretending to be so excited about Norman, but, well. You know. It still seemed like a *remote* possibility. I hadn't completely given up.

"I've been dumped before," Angela said. "It sucks. But you move on. You rip up some pictures and you move on."

"I don't think it'll be that easy for me," I said.

"I'll help," she said. "You can come hang out with me

tonight, if you want. I'll get the kids I'm babysitting into bed early, and we'll just hang out."

"Thanks," I said.

Nothing on *Full House* had ever prepared me for this. There were no hopeless gay crushes on that show, to start with. And the breakups were always really healthy. D. J. and her boyfriend walked up a mountain, broke up, and walked back down, and that was that. Danny's fiance moved to New York and he was over her two episodes later. No one ever got all the juice squeezed out of their heart.

"Come on," said Angela. "Lunch is over. Fifth period is starting up."

I shook my head at her. "No way." I said. "I'm not leaving. Not yet."

"You want me to stay with you?" she asked.

I shook my head again. "Leave me alone, please."

"Fine," she said. "But I'm coming to check on you. I'll tell Mrs. Vanderbilt I have to go and that I might be a while. Okay?"

I nodded. At least *someone* gave a damn about me. Angela had even offered to skip class to be with me, which was really cool of her.

She walked out. I locked the door of the stall, and I was left alone.

A few minutes later, I was officially skipping a class for the first time in my life. It felt like I had taken the first step on the road to a life of crime.

And it was the best I'd felt all day.

✴ Four ✴

After about twenty minutes, I was calming down a little bit. I'd cried out everything inside me that was there to cry out. I'd even taken, like, a ceremonial pee so I could get *that* out of me along with all the snot, tears, and other gunk that was coming out. I symbolically flushed away every bit of the "old Debbie" that I could force out into the toilet along with the chastity ring.

For several minutes after I pulled my pants back up, I sat there not thinking anything or feeling anything. The grapefruit that was my heart had been squeezed of its last drop of juice.

Finally, I thought about my options for the rest of the day. Where could I go next? I certainly wasn't going back to class. Not that period, anyway.

But I knew that I definitely had to confront Lisa, and fast, even though it was probably hopeless. If not, I'd just have another breakdown every time I saw her.

The best scenario I could imagine would be for it to happen that night, in the parking lot outside the movie theater. Maybe Norman would try to go up Lisa's shirt during the movie and she'd get all upset that he was trying to go too far. She'd storm out and try to tearfully call me for a ride home, and I could say, "I'm already here, Lisa! Look up!" And she'd look up, and there I'd be, standing in the rainy parking lot holding up my phone so she could see the glowing screen, a light waiting to carry her home.

That would be awesome.

But it still sounded like the stunning conclusion to the season finale of a TV show, not real life. More likely, I'd just build up the nerve to talk to her right before the movie, on the way in, and she'd get all freaked out and I'd have another breakdown over by the box office. By the time I made it home, I'd be calling Dad to see if I could go live with him and not have to look Lisa in the eye anymore.

Five minutes later, Angela showed back up in the bathroom.

"Debbie?" she called.

I stood up from the toilet and stepped out of the stall.

"Hey," I said, weakly.

"Jesus, Deb," she said. "You look like crap."

I shrugged and sat down against the wall. She sat down and joined me.

"I never would have guessed you had a thing for Lisa," Angela said. "Even though it was pretty obvious, now that I think about it."

"She never would have guessed either," I said. I sniffed, trying to get some snot back into my nose. Some of it had already gotten onto my white shirt.

Broken hearts are fucking gross.

I *almost* said that out loud.

"Somewhere in the back of my head, I thought that Lisa and I would be together forever in a house with a white picket fence, three kids, and hilarious neighbors."

"Everyone gets caught up in that modern day fairy-tale shit," said Angela. "It's programmed into our brains from day one."

"Everyone talks about how TV desensitizes kids to sex and violence and the A-word, but they never stop to think how badly you can be screwed up by stuff like *Full House*."

Angela laughed and pulled a couple of cigarettes out of her purse. "Smoke?"

Now, look, I may have been a very stupid person— we've pretty much established that at this point—but I wasn't about to get into smoking. Right at that moment, though, it seemed like just the thing to do.

"Give me one," I said.

It was something the old Debbie never would have

done, but having a cigarette meant that I would set fire to something. It could be, like, a symbolic burning away of everything that came before. I'd never have to smoke another one after this.

Angela lit her cigarette, then handed me one and flicked the lighter in front of me. I took a puff and then proceeded to hack up a pretty good portion of my lung.

Sheesh. More stuff to get out from the inside of me.

I felt as though any minute now, Nancy Reagan or some other special guest star would burst into the room to warn me about the dangers of smoking and teach me to say no. It would be a very special episode of *Debbie Woodlawn's Stupid Life*.

Well, no. I wouldn't have my own show. It would be a very special episode of *The Wonderful World of Lisa* that focused on a character who was being written out of the series soon. Maybe they'd kill me off to teach everyone else a lesson.

Angela politely ignored the cough instead of laughing at me. I didn't keep trying to smoke, though. I just held the cigarette. I'd already set fire to something.

"Love sucks," Angela said, exhaling.

"Yeah," I said. "I can't believe Lisa said she's okay with people doing more than kissing before they get married. We just went to an abstinence rally in Omaha a few months ago. And there were people there who do that courtship thing where they never even *touch* until the wedding, and she thought it was cool."

"She probably never felt this way before," said Angela. "You can't fight hormones that well in real life. Lots of people in ACTs think girls who go past first base are sluts until they actually get a boyfriend themselves. Then they find out it's harder than they thought."

I just sighed and watched the thin plume of smoke rise from the end of the cigarette.

"Look," Angela said. "I know how bad what you're going through sucks. Like you want to crawl into a snakehole and tear off every bit of your skin and set what's left of you on fire."

"Yeah," I said. "I already symbolically flushed myself down the toilet."

Angela laughed. "Well, that's a start," she said. "If you want my advice, you need to just find a random girl and a comfortable back seat where you can work off some steam."

"I don't think I know a single other gay girl in school," I said. "Except for those ones who hang out in the drama hall."

"Half of them are faking it," said Angela. "And some of them are really mean, too."

"I guess I could just close my eyes and sleep with Nate Spoelstra," I said.

"Yeah," said Angela. "Uh, don't do that. He's so greasy you'd end up feeling like you were on a Slip-n-Slide."

I managed a weak smile. Or half of one, anyway.

We sat in silence for a minute while Angela took a few more thoughtful drags on her cigarette.

"Why do you go to ACTs, anyway?" I asked. "Do you believe in all that stuff?"

She took another puff and shrugged. "Some of it, I guess," she said. "I started going because of a guy, though."

"Which one?"

"Ryan Hart," she said slowly, as if the words felt funny in her mouth. "You know him?"

Ryan was one of the thirty or so people who showed up at an ACTs event once in a while, adding to the dozen or so who showed up for every meeting and event, like Lisa and me. I think he floated back and forth between ACTs and the Fellowship of Christian athletes.

"Sure," I said. "He's pretty nice."

"I used to think he was, too," Angela said. "So I started following him around. After a while I got the idea that even if we actually started going out, he'd trade me for football tickets in a heartbeat, so I got over him and moved on to another guy. But my parents were so pumped that I was going to ACTs that I just can't bring myself to quit."

"Makes sense," I said.

She took another few puffs, then said, "I have to get back to class. You coming?"

"Next period," I said. "I'm gonna sit the rest of this one out."

"Cool," she said. "Seriously, though, come by the

Santonis' tonight if you want. I'll text you the address. I'll be there at seven, and the kids are in bed by nine"

"I'll try," I said. "I may need to just go nuts tonight."

"I'll make sure there's something to drink," she said with a smile. "And I'll try get something better to smoke."

I wasn't sure I was ready for drinking and drugs or whatever, but if talking to Lisa didn't work out—and I was bracing myself that it almost definitely wouldn't—I'd be up for anything. I'd probably *need* something strong. But I was glad I at least had somewhere to go, someone to see. That was a relief.

Before Angela left, she turned back to me. "Hey, do you know Emma Wolf?" she asked.

"That's the girl who was in the bathroom with us this morning, right?"

"Yeah. If she talks to you again, let her talk."

"Why? So she can tell me about her cult or whatever?"

"It's not exactly a cult, from what I understand," said Angela. "She and that Tim guy have this made-up religion or something, but I don't think they sacrifice virgins to the devil or pray to Elvis or anything. If you're looking to go nuts, she can probably help you better than I can."

"Okay."

She ground her cigarette out against the wall, tossed the butt in the trash, and left, leaving me by myself again. I shouldn't say I was feeling better, because I wasn't, but I think I'd about cried myself out, at least for the moment. I wouldn't have to see Lisa or Norman again for a few hours, at least. I could try to put them out of my mind and just worry about the future.

Things were going to be different, no matter what.

People in ACTs tended to make a big deal about being "born again." After the meetings, when I got home and there was no one around to read my mind, I'd think it was all stupid. I'd gotten birth right on the first attempt.

Then again, my mom had been doing all the work when I was born, and she doesn't get much right the first time. Maybe I really did need to do it all over again. I decided that when I got around to emerging from the depths of the restroom, I was going to be emerging as a whole different person, like the stall had been a second womb.

I looked down at the cigarette I was still holding—it had burned most of the way down now, and there was a long stream of ash hanging on for dear life on the end of it, which looked kind of cool.

I put the cigarette out on the floor and made sure it was really, really out so I could throw it in the trash without setting a fire, then walked back into the stall. I sat back down on the toilet for a minute so that if anyone from the faculty came in, I could make it look like the cigarette hadn't been mine. I didn't want to get detention or anything.

Then it hit me. Detention! I didn't want to spend the afternoon alone, and I was going to need some new friends anyway. Every time someone on TV gets detention, they make new friends there.

I'd never had a detention in my life.

But that was *old* Debbie.

I *wasn't* the old Debbie anymore, the one who was just a recurring character on *The Wonderful World of Lisa*. That Debbie got flushed.

Even if I ended up getting Lisa to say "yes" and we became an actual couple, I was going to be a co-star, not a sidekick.

This would be my first day as a new person.

If someone on *Full House* wanted to get baptized, but the family couldn't get to the church or wherever because they were locked in some sort of big public restroom for some reason, they'd roll up their sleeves, get everyone else together, and give the person the best darned baptism the town had ever seen, right there in the bathroom.

I'd already symbolically flushed myself away and burned myself up. Now I walked to the sink, splashed water on my face, and gave myself the best darned baptism I'd ever had.

✳ Five ✳

People in ACTs liked to say that the whole world changes for you when you "get saved."

I'm not sure how any of the people in ACTs knew this, exactly, since I think they'd all been born into their religion, but I could sort of see what they meant when I stepped out of the bathroom.

The hall seemed different to me than it had before. The people didn't seem so strange or intimidating. I felt … calm, in a way. Or detached, I guess. I don't know. Anyway, I felt a bit different, which is what I needed to feel most.

Fifth period—gym—wasn't the best place to try to get detention. People acted up in there all the time, and Mr. Ward never did anything. I made an excuse about having a headache and spent the whole class sitting in the bleachers.

But Mrs. Goldfarb, my sixth period teacher, was an easier target. She wasn't exactly a strict disciplinarian, but she wasn't hard to shock, either. When they started up the thing with uniforms, she and Mrs. Smollet, the guidance counselor, lobbied hard for it to require girls to wear dresses. She was *that* sort of teacher.

I found my way into her class way before the late bell rang, sat down, and put my feet up on my desk, which was strictly against the rules. Goldfarb didn't seem to mind too much when guys put their legs up, but she thought it was "unladylike" for girls.

When she saw me, she sort of glared at me, then pointed down at the ground, to indicate that I should put my legs back below the desk, but I ignored her, hoping to egg her on.

Mrs. Goldfarb walked over to me. "Debbie!" she whispered. "Putting your legs in that position is not entirely modest."

"Probably not," I said.

She stared at me for a second. "This isn't like you at all, Debbie," she said.

"I know," I said. And she shrugged her shoulders and just walked back to her own desk.

Great. My first attempt at acting up, and I was getting away with it!

Eventually I did put my legs down, because besides

being "not entirely modest," it was also not entirely comfortable.

I spent most of the rest of class trying to get my nerve up to try getting in trouble again. A few times I raised my hand for just a second, then chickened out and put it back down. Finally, with ten minutes left to go in class, I put my hand in the air and kept it there.

"Yes, Debbie?" Mrs. Goldfarb asked, pointing at me.

I froze for a second, then summoned all the courage I could fake and opened my mouth.

"I have to take a piss," I said.

A bunch of people snickered. Mrs. Goldfarb looked totally shocked.

"Debbie!" she said. "What did you just say?"

I blushed, and built up my nerve again.

"I said I have to take a damn piss!" I said.

Now everyone really cracked up. I blushed more, since I imagined that they were all picturing me doing what I said I had to do.

"Debbie, come here!" said Mrs. Goldfarb. I got up and walked over to her desk, careful not to look anyone in the eye.

"What's gotten into you today?" she asked. "Are you all right?"

"I'm fine," I said with a shrug. "I just have to piss."

"You know that I don't tolerate that sort of language in class," she said. "Especially out of young ladies such as yourself. It's entirely inappropriate."

"That's totally unfair," I said. "If it's okay for guys, then it should be okay for girls, too."

"I didn't say it was okay for guys," she said. "I'm going to let it slide this time, but please be more prudent in the future."

"All right," I said.

I almost added "You fat old wrinkled pumpkin-head," but I couldn't quite build up the nerve to go that far.

Man, this was going to be harder than I thought. Apparently going through almost three years of high school without causing any trouble gives you a sort of buffer zone that's hard to break through when you need a detention.

When the bell rang, everyone else jumped up and ran out of class to start up their spring break. I hadn't thought of anything else that would get me into trouble with Mrs. Goldfarb that I had the guts to do. And now the day was over. I'd failed.

But as I walked through the hall with the crowd of happy people, past the bathroom where I'd had my symbolic rebirth, it suddenly occurred to me that they probably didn't give you tickets to get into detention or anything. If I just showed up, uninvited, I could *say* that I was supposed to be there, and they wouldn't be able to do anything about it. They'd probably let me in.

So I turned right around and walked my way down to room 320—the detention room—and stepped inside.

I'd never seen the inside of that room before; for all I

knew, the people inside might all be wearing leather jackets or tight mini-skirts and fishnets. Honestly, that's sort of what I was expecting.

But the detention room was just a regular classroom, the one they'd used for study hall back when there was such a thing as study hall. And not one of the six kids inside looked like a greaser or a prostitute or anything—except maybe Hairy Nate, who was sitting at one of the desks picking at his fingernails. He sort of leered at me when I came in.

Emma Wolf—the weird girl who'd been in the bathroom with Angela, knew about my feelings for Lisa, and tried to sell me a new religion for five bucks—was there, along with Tim, the gay guy she'd been sitting with at lunch. The only other three people in the room were two Outdoor Kids and a goth.

Emma was busily scribbling in a notebook. Tim sat next to her, wearing a shirt that said *Reebok* in iron-on letters. The first week we were allowed to iron on letters, a few kids tried writing the names of brands or singers on their shirts, but they mostly ended up feeling stupid. Tim's was the first I'd seen in months that just said a brand name. Maybe it was supposed to be ironic or something.

I didn't really want to hear about their religion, but I sat down directly in front of Emma. Angela had vouched for her, after all. I could at least give her a chance.

At the head of the room sat a bald teacher I didn't

recognize. When I sat down, he looked at me and said, "Name?"

"Debbie Woodlawn," I said.

"And who sent you here?"

"Mrs. Goldfarb," I said.

"First-time offender?"

I nodded.

The bald-headed teacher said, "You will be here until three p.m. exactly, and until then there is to be no talking, only quiet study and reflection on your behavior and ways in which you can improve. If you are sent here three times, you will be assigned a session with a guidance counselor. Any questions?"

"Nope."

He nodded, and I made myself as comfortable as I could at the desk. A few seconds later, I felt a tap on my shoulder, turned around, and Emma passed a note up to me.

> Do you feel lost? Confused? Alone?
> Circle One: Yes or No.

I would have ignored it normally, but I wasn't there to ignore people.

I circled "yes" and passed it back to her.

I heard her scribble some more, then she passed up another note.

> The Church of Blue can help you.
> We are not a cult—don't worry.

Nothing all that weird. Five dollars for a holy quest is a good deal. Trust me.

Giving someone five bucks to tell me about their religion was the dumbest idea I'd ever heard. People who want to be your friends don't ask you for money up front, normally, unless it's a sorority or whatever.

But right about then, I was desperate. Anything that might keep me from having to spend the rest of the day alone, killing time until Norman and Lisa's date, was worth a shot. I'd chicken out for sure if I didn't have anyone to cheer me on.

There was a problem, though. I didn't have a dime in my pocket, let alone five bucks.

So I wrote her a note of my own.

I'll give you five bucks. But I don't have any cash—do you have five bucks I can borrow?

I heard Emma chuckle triumphantly when I passed it back to her, and a second later she passed me a five dollar bill, which I passed right back to her.

Tim started humming "Ode to Joy."

Emma scribbled for a second, then passed me another note.

Meet me after detention, and you will learn the secrets of the Church of Blue and begin a holy quest.

I wrote another one back.

Okay. I'm in the mood for a crazy scheme, as long as I end up at the movie theater tonight. I need to talk to Lisa.

She took the note and passed me another a second later.

Praise be to you Kimmy Gibbler, Patron Saint of wacky neighbors and crazy schemes.

1, 2, 3, 4…

✶ Six ✶

Okay. Deep breath.

Obviously, she had just heard about the *Full House* thing from Angela, right? She couldn't *really* read my mind. No one could, and no religion gave you magic powers. I mean, even the Wiccan kids couldn't do that sort of stuff, and they weren't just making their religion up on their own.

Right?

But Emma already *knew* my biggest secret. The worst thing she could find out by reading my mind now was that I thought she was probably full of crap.

Through the rest of detention, I kept sneaking glances back at Emma and Tim, trying to tell if they were serious just by looking at them. Emma was pale and kind of dumpy looking. Tim was scrawny, just about equally pale, and wearing a dirty pair of glasses. His blond hair looked like it had never seen a comb. For a gay guy, he was sort of shockingly unfabulous.

Another religion to deal with may have been just about the last thing I wanted, but I was determined to at least get my money's worth, and even hanging out with freaky mind readers sounded better than being alone. When detention ended, I turned around to talk to them.

"Hi," I said.

"Hey," said Emma. "I'm Emma Wolf. This is my first disciple, the Apostle Tim."

I smiled and nervously shook both of their hands.

"So, what's it all about?" I asked. "What do you guys believe in?"

"It's not a question of what we *believe* so much as what we've managed to figure out so far," said Emma.

"Well, *make up* so far," said Tim.

"Right," said Emma. "We both needed a higher power to call on to help us get over bad habits, but neither of us was into any of the religions we knew about, so we made up our own."

"And now we're going on a holy quest?" I asked.

"That's the best way to introduce someone to Bluedaism," said Emma. "Take them on a holy quest."

"We think so, anyway," said Tim. "No one ever gave us five bucks before."

"What kind of holy quest are we talking about?"

"I don't know yet," said Emma. "Every holy quest is different. You have any requests?"

I decided to be honest with her. I mean, she already knew my biggest secret. I didn't have much left to hide.

"I'm trying to build up the courage to talk to Lisa tonight," I said. "Like, declaring myself or whatever. And I'm getting ready to re-start my whole life and move to Minneapolis when she rejects me."

Emma turned to Tim. "She's in love with her best girlfriend," she explained. "And she's in ACTs."

"Ouch," said Tim.

Damn, I still couldn't get over how weird it felt to actually hear people say that stuff out loud.

"When were you going to talk to her?" Emma asked.

"After her date with Norman. That's why I need to be at the theater."

"Perfect," said Emma. "We have some time to kill, then."

We started walking down the hall.

"So, what were you in for?" asked Tim.

"I didn't do anything," I said, continuing my plan to just be honest. I didn't really have the energy to think up a good lie, anyway. "I just thought it would be a good way to meet new people."

"Hallelujah!" said Tim. "That's why we went, too!"

"Well," said Emma, "come on out to my car and we'll get this thing started. If you need something to keep you occupied 'til the whole thing with Lisa, we've got you covered."

"Thanks," I said. "I really don't want to be alone today."

Just as we got to the front door, a voice came from down the hall.

"*Wolf!*" it shouted.

I turned around to see Heather Quinn walking toward us.

Heather was kind of a lower-tier "popular" girl. Not exactly well-liked, but well-known, at least. She wasn't a cheerleader or student body president or anything, but she was on homecoming court, and joined so many clubs that the yearbook was practically a photo spread of her. She was short—probably not even five feet tall—but cute.

"Sorry Heather," Emma shouted. "We have to go!"

"Don't you dare, Wolf!" shouted Heather as she stomped up the hall toward us. "This ends *today*!"

Emma turned to me. "Run," she said casually.

And she took off running like hell down the side hall.

"You think *you* can outrun me?" Heather called.

Tim and I followed Emma. Half of me wanted to just stay put and keep out of someone else's fight, but for the moment, I was on Emma and Tim's team.

We ran down the hall, then down the next one, then ducked into the school newspaper office. I heard Heather behind us, calling Tim's name out.

"Get in here," said Emma. "There's a back exit."

We ran through the office and out a back door that

took us to the staff parking lot. As soon as we got outside, Emma slumped against the wall, breathing heavily. She looked like she was almost hyperventilating—she wasn't exactly in great shape for running that fast, obviously.

"Think we lost her?" asked Tim.

Emma nodded. "She's not on the paper," she said. "She probably won't know about the door."

She forced herself back up and started walking out into the parking lot. Tim and I followed.

"What was that all about?" I asked. "You didn't, like, kill her family or anything, did you?"

"Know how we told you we were in detention to meet people?" Emma asked between breaths.

"Yeah," I said.

"That was only half true. We also had to hide out from Heather," said Emma.

"She tends to get pranked during a lot of holy quests," said Tim. "She usually doesn't find out it was us. I guess she did today."

"We like to mess with her because she was mean to us in middle school," said Emma. "You ever hear that rumor that Tim was gay?"

"Yeah," I said. "Aren't you?"

Tim shook his head. "Not that there's anything wrong with it, but that's just a rumor Heather started a few years ago that won't die. And she used to call Emma a sea otter or something."

"Manatee," grumbled Emma. "She called me a manatee. Which is also known as a sea *cow*."

The parking lot was almost empty now—everyone had taken off after school. But off in the distance, at the edge of the lot, I could see an old, beat-up blue car that I just sort of instinctively knew was going to turn out to be Emma's.

"What prank do you think she found out about, anyway?" Tim asked.

"The one a few weeks ago," said Emma. "The dictionary one."

"That was a stupid one," said Tim. "Because she's totally not fat."

"Yeah, I know she's still only about half my size, but I swear to Blue, she's put on weight!" Emma turned to me. "And since she was getting chubbier, I put pictures of her into every dictionary in school next to the word 'fat.'"

"Who even cares if she's putting on weight?" asked Tim. "She still looks fine."

Emma scowled. "Whatever," she said, standing up. "It wasn't even part of a holy quest."

"Well, obviously there was nothing holy about it."

"Can we just get going? She's bound to figure out that we slipped outside sooner or later."

We walked all the way out to the beat-up old blue sedan, just like I expected we would. The car looked as though it hadn't been cleaned in a while, and like it had gone for a drive in an acid rainstorm or something.

Emma and Tim got in the front seats, and I let myself into the back.

"Pardon the mess," said Emma. "Just push the crap out of your way."

"Okay."

Stepping into Emma's car was the first time I got the idea that going somewhere with the two of them might not be the safest thing I'd ever tried. I mean, I knew it could be trouble, but I didn't realize that I might be putting myself in physical danger.

All through the car, there were empty cans of energy drinks and paper bags from the Burger Box—some of which probably had strands of Nate Spoelstra's hair inside of them, since he worked there—and then there was a large pile of laundry, a couple of board games, at least three backpacks, a trumpet, a bunch of Neighborhood Watch signs, enough sheets of paper to open an office supply store, and a few rusty pots and pans. And this was just the stuff I could see—if you cleared away the mess, there might have been some body parts in there, for all I knew. It certainly smelled bad enough. How did I know they weren't going to cut me up into tiny pieces and keep me in the trunk?

I didn't even want to *think* about what might be in the trunk.

On the dashboard was a little hood ornament or Buddha, or whoever that fat laughing bald guy you see in Chinese restaurants is, with a spring attached to his butt.

I don't know what color it was to start with, but it had been sort of sloppily painted blue. Emma and Tim both patted its head as they got in.

"Check out the roof," Emma said. I looked up to see several large holes. "A few more years and this thing's going to be a convertible. Only it won't be able to convert back to having a roof.

"Emma hasn't cleaned the car since she got it," Tim explained, turning back. "And we have to keep it stocked with whatever we might need for holy quests."

"Tim was a Cub Scout," said Emma. "He likes to be prepared."

"So you drive around with rusty cookware?" I asked.

"You never know what might come in handy on a holy quest," said Emma. "We could end up in another country by the time this night is up! You know Canada is only, like, nine hours from here? We could have breakfast there if we took off *now.*"

"We don't have the gas money to drive nine hours, though," said Tim. "Just that one five dollar bill."

"And we couldn't make it back in time for me to see Lisa tonight," I said.

"I'm just saying, is all," said Emma. "If we had the time and money, we could go to Canada tonight. Nothing stopping us but the border guard. And when we needed to cook up some beans by the side of the road in Manitoba, you'd be glad we had the cookware."

Tim started to cough. "But we'd better at least get out of *here*, now."

Heather Quinn had made it out of the back door and was marching toward us.

Emma started up the car and drove out of the parking lot and into the streets of the neighborhood behind the school. We barely got half a block before she came to an open garage and pulled in.

"You live this close, but you drive to school?" I asked.

"I don't live here," she said. "This is Jim the Janitor's house. We can hide out here for a few minutes while we tell you about Bluedaism."

"Jim's a cool cat," said Tim. "Sometimes when we need money, he pays us to hang fliers for his chimney sweeping business."

"And he doesn't mind if you use his garage for proselytizing?" I asked.

"I'm sure he'd be cool with it," said Tim. "Hell, I should shut the door. Then Quinn'll never find us."

"She's probably already driving around looking for us," said Emma. "Probably thinks we vanished into thin air."

Tim stepped out and hit a button on the wall that made the garage door go down, effectively hiding us from Heather.

I have nightmares about sneaking around in people's houses all the time. I was sure that any second someone would step into the garage and call the cops on us. But nothing happened.

Emma turned toward me as Tim climbed back into the car. "Now that we've escaped Quinn's evil clutches … where were we?"

"You were telling me how you made up a religion," I said.

"Right. So, we started hanging out together because no one else would, thanks partly to Heather," said Emma. "No one wanted to hang out with Fatty and Faggy."

Tim socked her in the arm. "I told you never to use that phrase again," he said.

She ignored him.

"Anyway," she went on, "in case you couldn't guess by looking at me, I have body issues. I used to have every eating disorder known to science. Then I found I could get a self-esteem boost by getting a random guy to have sex with me. And while I was doing that, Tim was drinking his weight in cheap booze every night. We both decided we needed to quit."

"One of the twelve steps in AA is acknowledging that some higher power can help you," said Tim. "So we made up The Church of Blue."

"We're Bluish," said Emma.

"Okay," I said. "So who's this Blue guy, anyway? The guy on the dashboard?"

"No, that's just Bluddha," said Emma. "Our good luck charm."

"Blue started out being Emma's car," said Tim. "But the car breaks down all the time, which means it kind of fails as a deity. So we started using 'Blue' as an all-purpose word for God, or magic, or love, or The Force, or whatever it is that runs the world. Anything cool that we can't explain. We got Bluddha so we'd have something to pat for luck."

"Okay," I said. "So what's it all about?"

Emma smiled. "God," she said, "I've been rehearsing this spiel forever and now I'm choking!"

"We've practiced this, but no one ever pays us so we never get to do it for real," Tim added.

"See, it's like this," Emma said. "We think that something like magic is real, and anyone who doesn't believe it can just go listen to side two of the Beatles' *Abbey Road* record. Humans can't create something that perfect without some sort of divine assistance. Some people call it 'magic.' Some people call it 'God.' We call it 'Blue.'"

"If you want to call it something else, that's cool, but it might make things a bit confusing," said Tim.

I nodded. This didn't seem too freaky so far. They hadn't told me to start eating more figs or buy a set of robes or anything.

"We think that everyone has their own version of magic, which we call a Spark of Blue, inside them," Emma went on. "It's what makes great artists, leaders, and scientists great. And if you work with people whose version of it compliments yours, you can become, like, greater than the sum of your parts. Some people are just meant to fit together."

"Like the Beatles," said Tim. "That's what made them so much better than every other band, even though most of their solo albums are just okay."

"Right," said Emma. "Their Sparks of Blue were complimentary, so when they played together, they were greater than the sum of their parts."

I nodded some more and imagined a glowing blue sparkly thing inside me, in between my lungs or something. And I imagined it glowing brighter when Lisa was nearby.

"That doesn't sound too crazy," I said. "How can you tell if someone has a spark that compliments yours?"

Emma shrugged. "If you create *Abbey Road* with someone, you'll know."

"And that's pretty much the long and short of it," said Tim. "We figure we ought to keep it sort of loose. People can join up without renouncing their other religions or anything."

"Yeah," said Emma. "You can be a Christian Bluist. Or a Blue Jew, which is cool because it rhymes."

"Or a Bluddhist?" I asked.

"Yeah!" said Emma. She gave Bluddha a push, and he wobbled around on his spring.

"Now, we do have some rules, commandments, and stuff like that which we've made up to flesh the whole thing out," she said. "It's just good business."

"Like what?" I asked.

"Here," said Emma. And she handed me a sheet of paper.

Ten Commandments of the Holy Church of Blue

1. Matters of the heart come first. Especially someone else's heart.

2. Be thou not an asshole. This is the point of all religion. Everything else is just commentary. But exceptions can be made for people who deserve it.

3. Goest thou on holy quests—do amazing things. Silly, helpful, and seemingly pointless things are also acceptable.

4. Taketh thou any detours or side trips or odd suggestions that come up, for they will lead thee to knowledge, and to adventure, and bring thee closer to Blue.

5. Never put thy words in the mouth of Blue. Thou knowest not what sort of Spark of Blue is inside of thee, or what sort is inside of others. The entire Church of Blue is an educated guess. Remember this. Don't get cocky.

6. *Floss thy fucking teeth. Thou only getteth one set.*

7. *Weareth thou no garment that costeth thou more than a tank of gas.*

8. *Thou Shalt Not maketh thy home in Nebraska (Nebraska is Bluish hell).*

That all seemed okay—especially the Nebraska part. I'd driven all the way through Nebraska with Lisa once on the way to an ACTs Jamboree in Denver. Once you get past Omaha, driving through Nebraska is probably the single most mind-numbingly boring thing a person can possibly do. Other than hanging out with Norman Hastings.

God, making that drive *with* him would probably create, like, a black hole on the interstate.

Still, I couldn't help but notice that there weren't exactly ten commandments on the list.

"That's only eight," I said, handing the paper back to Tim.

"Yeah," said Emma. "We left a couple blank to fill in later when we think of something good. Or if some Blue dude comes out of the sky with tablets."

"We were already really stretching for a couple of them, anyway," said Tim. "Emma's shoes cost way more than a tank of gas."

"But these aren't shoes," said Emma. "They're an orthotic support system. In fact, maybe we should change it to say 'never wear a pair of shoes without proper arch support unless thou wanteth thy feet to hurt.'"

"That's not much of a commandment," said Tim.

"No," Emma agreed. "But, what the hell. We're on a holy quest. We might come up with another one today."

"So, do you guys, like, believe in all this for *real*, or what?" I asked.

"Well, we just made it up to help us stay out of trouble," said Emma. "But I swear to Blue, it works. Tim hasn't had a drink in months."

"And Emma hasn't had sex with anyone lately, instead of five people a week."

"Five a week?" I asked.

"He's exaggerating," said Emma.

Tim looked back and mouthed, "I'm not."

"Look, I had a problem," said Emma. "Not that I think sex is a problem, because I totally don't, but you shouldn't just do it to feel better about yourself, which is what I was doing, and it wouldn't have kept me eating normally forever. And keeping Tim out of trouble gives me something else to feel good about."

"I'm kind of the opposite of you guys," I said. "I sort of feel like I need to be *less* well behaved. I still feel weird when I swear out loud. I don't even watch TV shows or read books that I don't think Lisa's family would approve of. I've spent the last five or six years living like a *Full House* character."

"Blue can help with that," said Emma. "It's not like our holy quests are all exactly on-the-level or anything."

"So what do you think?" Tim asked me. "We've told you the basics. You ready for a quest?"

"I guess so," I said. "As long as I'm back by the time Lisa and Norman go to the movies."

"Then let us begin!" said Emma.

✳ Seven ✳

Tim got the garage door open and then got back in
the car. Emma started her car up but didn't take
off. Instead, she just turned on the stereo.

"We always open with a hymn," she said.

"Do I have to sing?" I said. I'm not much of a
singer. When we sang in ACTs, I always just moved my
lips and pretended.

"Oh, don't worry," said Emma. "Tim's not even
allowed to sing, because I care about my ear drums. We
just listen to the hymns."

"They're mostly classic rock songs," said Tim. "Plus
some Arcade Fire and White Stripes and stuff."

"What makes them hymns, then?" I asked.

Emma smiled. "Ah, young apostle," she said, "you have a lot to learn."

This annoyed me a bit. Not only had I never decided to be an apostle in the first place, but she hadn't answered my question. I really hate it when people make fun of you for asking stupid questions, but don't answer them. Like, when I was eight or nine I asked my dad if there were tarantulas in Iowa. He snickered and said, "Oh, yeah, they're the size of lawn mowers. We get them all the time. Your cousin Tyler was eaten by one." He made me feel stupid for asking, and I still didn't know if I should be on the lookout for tarantulas.

Emma told Tim to go lower the garage door back down (not all the way, so we wouldn't die of fumes) and turn out the lights, because everyone knows that music sounds better in the dark. Once it was darker, she fumbled around with her stereo, then started playing a song that opened up with an acoustic guitar riff.

"This is Bob Dylan," she said. "One of our holy prophets."

"There are three holy Bobs," said Tim. "Dylan, Marley, and Hope."

"We sometimes say 'Bob' as a synonym for God," said Emma. "And "Nebraska" was probably an Indian word that meant 'damn it,' so 'Bob Nebraska' is a Bluish way of saying 'God damn it.'"

The acoustic guitar turned out not to be just the opening riff; it turned out to be the only instrument, and

Bob Dylan turned out to be a guy who sounded like he was singing out of his nose. It sounded nothing like the contemporary Christian music that Lisa was into, except for the fact that it had a really repetitive rhythm that bugged me at first.

Repetitive songs always sort of annoy me. There was this one song Lisa listened to a lot that just went "I will praise him, I will praise him" over and over and over again. In the safety of my own room, I would think, "Man, quit *planning* to praise him and just do it already! Either pee or get off the pot!"

But this song wasn't repeating any one line over and over again. It wasn't repeating *any* lines—Bob was spitting them out one after another, so fast that I couldn't even keep track of them. One line about how anyone who's not busy being born is busy dying caught my ears, but then, before I could think about it, he was saying something else.

Plus, the longer we stuck around in someone else's garage, the more nervous I got. Even if Jim the Janitor *was* a friend of Emma and Tim, I didn't think he'd want us creeping around his garage.

And the song went on and on and on. Now and again I'd think the song was ending and we could finally leave, but then the guy would start singing again. And he was hardly even singing—"talking" was a better description of it. It was driving me nuts.

Tim and Emma, meanwhile, sat there very solemnly the whole time. I think they even had their eyes closed.

Right at the end of the song, though, there was a line that just about knocked me out of my seat. The rhythm slowed down just enough that I could tell he was about to say something important, and then he said that if his thoughts could be seen, people would probably put his head in a guillotine.

Damn. I knew how *that* felt.

Emma turned around as the song finally ended. "You like it?"

"It was … interesting," I said. "What was that thing about being busy being born?"

"He said that if you're not busy being born, you're busy dying," said Emma. "And that's the whole point of a holy quest—to get busy being born." Tim got the garage door back open and climbed into the car, and Emma pulled out onto the street and stepped on the gas, saying, "Praise be to Blue, and hallelujah!"

Tim looked out the window as we flew down the street. "I'll bet no one in heaven still says 'hallelujah,'" he said. "It's probably like saying 'gee golly' on Earth."

I chuckled for the first time in hours. "Where are we going, anyway?" I asked.

Emma slammed on the brakes and pulled over to the curb, in front of a yellow house with a bunch of little kids playing in the yard. The kids stopped and took a step backward, like they thought we were strangers who were going to offer them candy.

"Shit," she said. "I hadn't thought of that. I was just veering in the general direction of George the Chili King."

"We should at least get the checklist out," said Tim.

He opened the glove compartment and started digging around. "We have a checklist of things to do, see, or find on holy quests," he said. "Some of them are quests in and of themselves, and some are just things to do along the way."

"It's like playing Auto Bingo," said Emma.

Tim handed me a sheet of paper:

Holy Quest Goal Checklist

1. Find and play a "Love Tester" machine.

2. Locate a guy with the same name as a U.S. president and get his autograph.

3. Talk our way into getting to the top floor of the Principal Building (801 Grand).

4. Plant a pressed ham at a place patronized by old ladies (or at the governor's mansion).

I looked up from the list.

"What's a pressed ham?" I asked.

"It's where you press your butt cheeks up against a

window when someone's sitting on the other side," said Emma. "We've done it at an old lady place, but we should really hit the governor's mansion too."

I looked back down at the list.

5. Drink six shots of straight espresso each, in one sitting.

6. Find a waitress named Irene, Wanda, or Rhonda.

7. Go inside a teacher's house.

8. Acquire a statue of a monkey.

9. Find the grave of Tim's great-great-great-grandpa Harry.

10. Convince a guy with a bad comb-over to shave his head.

11. Find someone who has a Scottish accent.

12. Touch something from ancient Rome.

13. Pee in the 18th hole of the Waveland Golf Course.

14. Find a guy in a suit and tie at George the Chili King.

15. Shake hands with a bowler who has bowled a perfect 300.

16. Win a game of Bingo (and act all arrogant about it, like Bingo hustlers, yo).

17. Fill Heather Quinn's shoes with whipped, sour, or shaving cream.

18. See a naked person of each gender (live and in person) in the same place at the same time (hands off, Emma!).

19. Break something expensive.

20. Witness a girl-on-girl kiss in which at least one participant has never kissed a girl before (boy-on-boy also acceptable).

All but the last three on the list had check marks next to them.

"So you guys did all these things?" I asked.

"Yeah," said Emma. "That's actually our fourth list, too. Some of them take a while, but we meet interesting people, find interesting places, and do amazing things along the way."

"Some of these kind of seem like they're breaking the 'Don't be an A-hole' rule," I said.

"Maybe a little," said Emma. "But mostly it's being a jackass, not an asshole. There's a difference."

"Like when we stole all those Neighborhood Watch Signs," said Tim. "That sort of toes the line, but proving they didn't really *mean* anything seemed like a good idea at the time."

"And we're giving them back," said Emma. "Our holy quest for spring break is to find really cool places to put them up."

"What did you touch from ancient Rome?"

"They had some old Roman coins at the coin shop on Fleur Drive," said Tim. "That one was easy. The hardest one on that list was actually finding someone with a Scottish accent in Des Moines."

"I'll bet," I said. "No one emigrates to Iowa."

"That last one will work out perfectly," said Tim as he took the list back. "Debbie can kiss Lisa at the end of the night. Who's the patron saint of goal setting?"

"Christ, *I* don't know!" said Emma. "But blessed be the name of whoever the hell it is, huh? I'll bet we can do *all* of those last three things tonight."

"Anything can happen on a night when you finish off a holy quest checklist," said Tim. "Especially if you knock three of them off to get there."

"I don't know," I said. "To be totally honest, I think the odds that she'll end up kissing me tonight are about a million to one."

"Gotta have faith," said Tim. "Blue will provide."

"Still," I said. "Naked people? Where would you find those?"

"That's no problem," said Emma. "I mean, if the night is winding up and we haven't found any, Tim and

I will get naked behind a bush or something before you talk to Lisa and kiss her. I'd hate for either of you to have to see my fat ass, but we'll do what we have to. And then we'll find something to break."

"I'll survive," said Tim. "I saw already saw your ass when you planted the pressed ham at the coffee shop. I didn't die."

Emma laughed. "I think the old lady who was sitting at the window almost did. She sure screamed loud enough."

"I'm putting that goal on the next list, too," said Tim, "but this time the governor's mansion is a requirement, not an option."

"Look out, Governor Branstad!" said Emma.

"I still don't know," I said. "I've never even *seen* a naked guy before."

"Well, all the more reason, then," said Emma. "That's what it's all about, isn't it? Trying new things?"

"We're not saying it would straighten you out to see someone's shlong or anything," said Tim. "But seeing people naked is, like, a life experience thing that everyone ought to do."

"Whatever," I said. "Does it even count if I'm the one who sees the people? I'm not Bluish."

"Anyone coming along on the quest is qualified," said Emma.

I nodded. "As long as I can keep *my* clothes on."

"Oh, you totally can," Emma said. "We wouldn't make you do anything you weren't comfortable with. But if we cross off all three of these tonight, *anything* can happen. I'm willing to get naked to get us to that point."

"So, how much time do we have?" asked Tim. "You know when the movie they're gonna see starts?"

"Not off the top of my head," I said. "They had other stuff in the afternoon, but they were going to two of them, so they're probably at, like, seven and nine. Angela might know for sure. Let me call her."

I reached around behind me for my backpack—and felt nothing.

Oh, God.

I thought back and realized I hadn't had it in detention, either. Or in the class before. Or in the bathroom. I'd been in such a haze, and everyone else had been so much into spring break mode, that I hadn't even thought to pull out a text book. I must have left it at the lunch table when I ran out in a hurry.

I always do things like that. Lisa used to joke that I'd lose my butt if it wasn't attached.

My chest started to tighten. My guts felt like they were going to come climbing out of my throat. My breathing got really short. My backpack had my list of reasons why I was not just a wacky sidekick in it. Including The Big One. Which I had stupidly not written in code or something.

And now someone else had it.

"Oh, crud," I said, starting to shiver. "Oh, crud, crud, crud."

"What?" asked Tim.

"My backpack . . . I think I left my backpack at the lunch table! It had my phone . . . and a list of reasons why I'm not just like Kimmy Gibbler from *Full House* . . . "

"So, if whoever has the bag opens it, you're outed?" Tim asked.

I nodded. "If Norman reads it, he'll tell Lisa and everyone else in the world. And she might feel like she has to prove to him that she's not gay, too . . . "

If Lisa found out that I liked girls from *me,* she'd probably be okay with it, at least. I mean, I didn't think it was really likely that she'd turn out to be in love with me, too, but she wouldn't throw a Bible at me or anything. A couple of the ACTs sponsors thought that having gay marriage be legal in Iowa would be the end of the world, but Lisa said she didn't really have a problem with it. I don't think many of any of the kids in ACTs did.

However, if Norman had my bag, and he found out and told her before I could, he'd probably tell her not to hang out with me anymore. I *hoped* she'd have the sense to tell him to go to hell, but she was stuck so far up his butt she could barely see out.

Emma turned back to me and put a hand on each of my cheeks.

"Breathe," she said. "Just breathe a second. We have this under control."

I tried to breathe. It helped a bit. Hearing her speak

so confidently didn't exactly reassure me, but it kept me from going into total panic mode.

"Who do you think might have it?" asked Tim.

"Lisa probably picked it up after lunch," I said. "Do you have a phone I can use?"

Emma passed me a phone and I dialed Lisa's number, but there was no answer. Just her voicemail:

"Hi, this is Lisa. If you're being chased by a bear, hit the pound sign, then hang up and run in a zigzag pattern. Otherwise, leave a message."

The phone beeped, and I said, "Hi, Lisa, it's me, Debbie. I'm on a friend's phone. Do you have my backpack? Call me at this number, okay? I really need it back."

I thought maybe I could call Angela or something, since I needed to know if she knew what movies Lisa and Norman were seeing anyway, but I didn't know her number. Lisa's was the only one I really knew by heart. I mean, I never actually dial people's whole numbers. They're all saved in my phone.

I called my own phone, hoping that whoever had it would answer, but it went to voicemail, too.

"Can we just go to Oak Meadow Mills, where Lisa lives?" I asked, handing Emma her phone back. "Her mom might know where she is. And she might have dropped my bag off at her house."

"Perfect," said Emma. "And Quinn probably won't be heading that way, so it's extra perfect."

"Sounds like a quest has fallen right into our laps," said Tim. "The Quest for Debbie's Backpack."

"If Blue or whoever it is hid my backpack just so we could have a quest, I'm moving to Minnesota and starting my own damn religion," I said. "One whose whole purpose is to wage war on Bluists."

"We could use one of those," said Tim. "It'd be great if we could be oppressed a bit. It'd really bring Bluists together."

"All two of us, yeah," said Emma. "Don't worry, Deb. Blue wouldn't pull that kind of crap on you."

"Can we just go?" I asked.

"Of course."

And she took off through the streets of Cornersville Trace again, zooming past De Gama Park and into the "historic" part of town near the mall.

Soon we were in a neighborhood full of damp, dilapidated houses with Christmas lights still hanging from the trees, weeds growing around the foundations, and patches of leftover snow covering rusty toys by the curbs. This was my neighborhood. All of the old, tiny houses were sort of weird looking, and none of them looked like they belonged next to other ones. At the end of the road were some shops, like Sip Coffee and a lousy ice cream shop where all the stoners hung out.

Emma took a couple of sharp turns down side roads—Tim said they were "sudden bootlegger turns" that she took to throw off anyone who might be following us.

Bluddha swung violently back and forth on his spring, but the suction cup kept him stuck to the dashboard.

Pretty soon, we were out of the old downtown, then out of Cornersville Trace proper and into new subdivisions full of cul-de-sacs, which had sprung up where the corn fields that separated our town from Waukee and Grimes were when I was a kid.

The further west of the old part of town you get, the bigger and nicer the subdivisions and shops are. In Juniper Creek, the first subdivision you come to when you get past 82nd, the houses are fairly large, but not mansions or anything.

In Oak Meadow Mills, which is about four layers of subdivisions out, the houses are practically palaces. They're all a mixture of white siding and brick, and spaced wide apart so it seems like the houses all have some room to stretch out and relax. Every house looked like a dream house to me.

"Take a left down Spruce Lawn Drive," I said as we pulled in. "It's number 8162."

"I hate these neighborhoods," said Tim. "All the houses look alike."

"I *love* these houses," I said.

"To each his own, I guess," Tim replied. "Give me the old part of town."

"Those houses are tiny," I said.

"So?" Tim asked. "Who needs *this* much room?

Places with a lot of extra space always feel haunted to me. Even when they're brand new."

"Haunted?"

"My house is pretty big," said Tim. "And … I don't know. It always seems like there ought to be something filling the space. Every night when I turn out the lights, it gets so freaky that I run to my room like I'm running for my life."

"Me too!" said Emma. "I run upstairs like something's chasing me."

"And seriously," said Tim. "Oak Meadow Mills? Where are the oak meadows? Or the mills?"

"It's just a name," I said. "The idea is you're supposed to picture a beautiful meadow full of oak trees and babbling brooks and cider mills."

"Which they cut down to put up the houses," Tim said.

Emma slapped him on the arm. "Be nice!" she said.

"No they didn't," I said. "It was all cornfields before."

"See, Tim?" asked Emma. "These houses are way nicer than corn."

"I guess," said Tim.

I'd always thought of Oak Meadow Mills as heaven. It was clean, bright, open, and gorgeous. With easy access to a road that went right to Jordan Creek, a mall much nicer than the old one near the high school. It wasn't cramped and old and dirty, like my neighborhood.

Emma turned back to me as we pulled into the

driveway. "Are you just going to get your backpack, or talk to her if she's there?"

"Talk to her, I guess," I said. "If I see her, I'll have to do it. Even if she *has* my backpack, Norman might have looked through it earlier, for all I know. And he'll tell her."

"You want us to come up there with you?" asked Emma. "For moral support?"

I shook my head. "I have to do this one by myself."

"Okay," said Emma. "Which bedroom is Lisa's?"

"That one," I said, pointing up. "The top left."

"If you want us to leave, turn the lights off and on in there a couple of times," she said. "Otherwise, we'll be waiting out here for you."

"Thanks," I said. "And if I don't see you again, thanks for the ride."

"It's a matter of the heart," said Emma, giving me an encouraging smile. "Commandment number one."

"Go get her, Deb," said Tim. "And if you want to come out and break stuff and see naked people after, that's fine, too. You paid for it."

I reached forward to pat Bluddha, then opened the door and started the long walk from the back seat to the front porch.

✴ Eight ✴

It took every ounce of bravery I could muster—or fake—to ring the doorbell to Lisa's enormous white house. They had one of those novelty doorbells, the kind that plays "You Light Up My Life" instead of just going "ding dong."

It felt weird to ring the bell at all. I usually let myself in, just like Kimmy Gibbler always let herself into the Tanners' place.

Lisa's mom, Carla, answered the door.

"Hi, Debbie!" she said. "How are you?"

"Okay," I said, trying to sound upbeat and positive. "Is Lisa home?"

"No," she said. "She came by for a minute, but she went somewhere with Jennifer."

"Jennifer R or Jennifer P?" I asked.

"P, I think. Are you looking for your backpack?"

"Yes!" I said. "Did she have it?"

"I'm not sure," she replied. "But she said you left it at lunch and she was sending you an email about it. You want to come in? I'll see if I can get ahold of her."

"Okay," I said, stepping in.

Lisa's mom was a very pretty woman. Well, "pretty" maybe isn't the word. "Clean" is more like it. Her face looked like she didn't just scrub it, she sandblasted it. She couldn't have possibly looked any more different from *my* mom, who always looks like she'd just slept in a tanning bed. Some people think a tan looks healthy, but on my mom, it just makes her look like her skin is made of Fruit Roll-Ups.

But the inside of Lisa's house looked nothing like you'd expect from the outside, or from how clean her mom always was. It was almost as messy as Emma's car.

To call Carla Ashby a pack rat would be putting it very, very gently. There were newspapers stacked as high as my head—one that I noticed on the way in was dated three years ago. There were books all over, knick-knacks, junk, empty jars, and washed-out butter containers. And there were dishes stacked up everywhere. All clean, of course—she wasn't so messy as to leave dirty dishes out, but they owned about three times as many dishes as they had room for. She and Emma could have gotten all their junk together and started up an interfaith flea market or something.

Lisa didn't let most of her friends into the house—she was sort of ashamed at what a mess it was. But I always adored her mom for being so messy, because, in a way, she was kind of like me: she was trying to be what Lisa and the people at her church wanted her to be, and kind of failing at it.

"Sorry about the mess," said Carla. "I keep swearing that I'm going to get around to cleaning it soon. But…you know."

"Totally."

I sat down at the table, which was covered with stacks of books. In front of me was the Home Care section of her table library—a stack of books with titles like *Kill Your Clutter* and *Clean Crusade: Maintaining a Christian Home*. Next to those was a stack of books about how to quit smoking, and a full ashtray that served as proof that the books didn't work.

Now, it's not that Carla was the least bit trashy or anything—she took her domestic work very seriously, even though she kind of sucked at cleaning. She didn't get a lot of company, since Lisa never brought anyone but me over, but she was a wonderful hostess. The second I sat down, she shoved some books out of the way and put down a glass of iced tea and a Rice Krispies treat for me.

"How's everything at school, hon?" she asked. "Have you decided on a college yet?"

"Not yet," I said. "I probably won't even start looking until next year."

"It's never too early," she said as she lit up a cigarette and went back to looking for her phone. "We've been trying to talk Lisa into going to a nice private school on the East Coast someplace. She has the grades for it. But I think that'll be a losing battle now."

"How come?" I asked.

"Well, you know," she said with a smile. "She'll probably want to go where Norman goes. And he's going to Iowa State."

"Ah," I said.

I hadn't even thought about that. I'd been waiting to see what college Lisa chose, since I didn't really care too much where I went—my family didn't have any deep-running ties to any college sports teams or anything. The only brochures I'd seen were ones that my mom picked up from places like the Maharishi Vedic University and other schools where I could probably major in astral projection.

I'd rather major in pest control down at the Shaker Heights Institute of Technology.

"Have you guys talked to Norman much?" I asked.

"He's been out to dinner with us a couple times," she said. "He'd probably be an excellent provider for Lisa."

"Sure," I said.

"What do you think of him?"

I took a bite of Rice Krispie treat and chewed on it

while I counted to twenty-five in my head. I didn't want to, like, mentally pick a fight with her or anything.

"I don't know much about him," I said. "But he's not into drugs or anything, I guess."

Lisa's mom found her phone under a stack of magazines and tried to make a few calls while I ate the rest of my snack and drank my tea. It sounded like she wasn't getting ahold of anybody.

Regardless of what happened after I finally talked to Lisa, things were never going to be the same between her mom and me. And I knew Carla well enough by then that she was practically like a second mom to me. She'd never seemed like she was judging me or looking down on me or expecting me to live up to anything.

But even if, by some miracle, Lisa and I were officially girlfriend-and-girlfriend by the end of that night, her mom would become sort of like ... not an enemy, exactly, but someone we had to team up against. Someone we had to keep a secret from. I mean, I loved her mom to death, but she was still kind of old-fashioned when it came to gay rights and stuff.

And if my encounter with Lisa was a train wreck, there was a chance that I'd never see her mom again. Maybe we'd nod at each other from afar after graduation or something, but this would probably be my last time in their house.

"I just can't get anyone on the phone," she said.

"Lisa's phone is going right to voicemail, and I don't have a number for Norman or either of the Jennifers."

I was actually kind of relieved. I had been sort of nervous about why Lisa hadn't called me back. I mean, I didn't blame her for not answering a number she didn't recognize, but she should have at least checked the voicemail. If she wasn't answering her mom's calls, either, maybe she really just didn't have her phone turned on. It meant that it was nothing personal, at least.

Carla dialed one more number, then said, "Sorry. No one's answering."

"Thanks for trying," I said. "You mind if I go up to Lisa's room and check my email on her computer?"

"Not at all!"

I took a last gulp of the iced tea and headed up to Lisa's bedroom, which was pristine and uncluttered— Danny Tanner, the *Full House* neat freak, would have loved the place. I think part of the reason Lisa liked *Full House* so much was that she kind of dreamed of having a parent who was a neat freak. One of the few things I didn't like about her was how upset she got at her mom whenever she seemed less than perfect.

It was kind of overwhelming to go into Lisa's room. It smelled like her. The *Full House* DVD set was sitting under her little TV, and one of the beanbag chairs against the wall still had what was probably my butt print in it from the last time I was there. I thought of all the nights I'd slept on the floor, or even in her bed, coming so close to this one dream I had, where we were cuddled up close in soft cotton pajamas...

1, 2, 3, 4, 5...

Her pink leatherette appointment book was sitting on her desk, and I flipped through it a minute, but didn't see any phone numbers or addresses. I didn't think there would be—those were usually stored in her phone. There was nothing that indicated where she might be in the calendar part, either.

But on one sheet, she had written things like *Mrs. Hastings*, *Lisa Hastings*, and *Mrs. Lisa Hastings* over and over—every possible version of her would-be married name except for *Lisa Ashby-Hastings*. She was too traditional for that, I guess. That didn't bode well for me.

I turned on her computer monitor, signed her out of gmail, and signed myself in. She'd sent me an email, just like I'd hoped.

Hey Deb,

You okay? Angela said you were upset about something, but seemed better by the end of the day. Hope you're all right! We'll schedule some time just for the two of us soon, okay? BTW, in case you didn't notice, you left your backpack at lunch! Norman's going to swing by your house and drop it off with you on his way to FCA bowling after school. If no one's

*home, he'll give it to me tonight and I'll hang
on to it for you. See you soon!*

My vision was going blurry by the time I got to the last line.

Norman had my backpack.

It was official. My life was over.

I signed out of gmail, then picked up a little scrap of paper from Lisa's desk and wrote *I love you* on it in really tiny letters. I figured maybe I could hide it someplace in her desk, back behind a drawer or something, where she wouldn't find it for a long, long time. Maybe not ever. So, one way or the other, no matter what happened, I would have left a little mark. A little bit of myself.

I pulled out the bottom drawer of her desk, so I could put the paper underneath it, and that's when I saw it.

A box of condoms.

And it had been opened.

Now, if it had been one or two condoms in the drawer, I would have been able to tell myself that she just got them from that Condom Lady who comes to health class now and then, and kept them to use as a gag gift or as a prop in some ACTs skit or whatever. But the Condom Lady only passes out a few at a time—not entire boxes. A box could only mean one thing.

Lisa was thinking about having sex with Norman. There was no other reason she'd have a whole box of condoms sitting around.

And she hadn't even told me, her best friend, about it.

A few drops of juice that had re-formed in my heart dribbled their way out and trickled down through my arteries.

I looked at the box and saw that it was a pack of twelve, and I actually counted to see how many were in there.

Ten. Two were missing.

Why would she be thinking of doing it with Norman after all those years of pumping her fist and chanting "True love waits" at abstinence rallies? Maybe she bought them to give a couple to a friend. Angela, maybe.

Even if that was the case, though, she kept the rest.

I sat on her desk chair for a good five minutes, thinking everything over and trying to get ahold of myself and trying to keep a panic attack from coming.

It was becoming more and more apparent that even though I'd been telling myself I'd just tried to live like I was in an old family sitcom to be more like Lisa, I was the only one of the two of us who had *really* bought into that whole fairy-tale world.

Either that or the thought of sex with Norman, of all people, was arousing enough to make her instantly abandon every ideal she ever claimed to have.

I put the box and drawer back, made my way downstairs, and thanked Lisa's mom for the tea.

"Oh, you're welcome, Debbie," said Carla. "Say 'hi' to Lisa and Norman for me later if you run into them, okay?"

I looked her square in the face, feeling like I should

tell her that her squeaky-clean little girl wasn't as squeaky-clean as she'd always made herself out to be. She had condoms in her room.

But I didn't. I wasn't like that.

"I will," I said.

"And try to stay dry! Sounds like a heck of a storm is coming in."

As I walked out of the house, possibly for the last time, I felt like I was leaving a lot behind. Lisa's room, which felt more like home than my own room. Lisa's family, which was like a second family to me—one that lived in the gorgeous white house in the pretty neighborhood.

And my vision of Lisa as the totally innocent type.

That should have been the hardest thing in the world for me to leave behind, but, in another way, it also gave me hope. Maybe she would be more receptive to other things that didn't fit in with the ACTs view of how the world should be...like being with me.

As long as she didn't want a threesome. There was no way I was letting Norman Hastings see me naked, and I sure as hell didn't want to see him, even if seeing a naked guy was one of the stupid goals of the holy quest.

"Any luck?" Emma asked as I got back to the car. "You were in there a while!"

"No," I said. "She wasn't home. I just wanted to say good-bye in case I'm never there again."

"You will be," said Emma. "This is totally going to work out for you!"

"I hope so," I said, as she started the car back up. "But you'll never believe what I found in her room."

"Condoms?" asked Tim.

"Yeah," I said.

"No way!" Tim said. "I was just kidding!"

"There was a whole box in her desk," I said. "And two of them were missing from the box."

"You went digging through her desk?" Tim asked.

"I went up to her room to get my email."

"Was your backpack there, at least?"

"No, that's what the email was about. Norman has it."

"Oh, not good," said Tim.

"He's the last guy in the world I want reading that note," I said. "He was going to swing by my house on his way to FCA Bowling, but I'm sure my mom wasn't home, so he still has it. We've got to get to the bowling alley."

"Which one?" asked Tim.

I went pale again. "I don't know," I said. "Whichever one the FCA uses for bowling nights."

"Mid-Iowa Lanes," said Emma.

"You sure?"

"Trust us," said Tim. "We've ended up there on plenty of quests."

"It's the perfect place for one," said Emma.

I couldn't say anything but "huh" as we drove back down Spruce Lawn Drive. Mid-Iowa Lanes was kind of a dump. It didn't sound like a great place for a holy quest to me. Then again, I'll bet that all of Moses' followers thought the same thing about the desert every day for forty years.

Tim's phone rang, and he looked at the ID. "Debt collector," he said. "That's the fourth time these guys have called me today! I don't even owe anyone anything!"

"Probably just looking for information on some other deadbeat," said Emma.

Tim shrugged. "We should have a holy quest where the goal is to find these guys and beat them up."

Emma put on a song by another guy she said was a prophet, and as we drove along I tried to think about all of the Church of Blue stuff, if only to keep myself from picturing Lisa putting a condom onto Norman's thing.

Nothing seemed too wacky or out-there about the religion Emma and Tim had made up. It wasn't even so much a religion as just a way of looking at the world. I didn't think I'd ever heard side two of *Abbey Road*, but I sort of understood what Emma meant. Like, sometimes you can hear two good singers singing the same thing, and even if they do it exactly the same way, one of them might just have this certain … something … that makes her version way better.

I guess there's a fine line between "magic" and "style." And if "Blue" was what they called that line, and it could make Lisa love me back, then I was ready to follow it anywhere. Even to a bowling alley.

We rolled through Cornersville Trace, past the strip malls on Cedar Avenue and the Burger Box where Nate worked, and across Merle Hay Road, which put us inside the Des Moines city limits.

The further east you go on Cedar, the older the stuff you drive past gets. In Cornersville, Cedar Avenue is a street full of sparkling new shops. On the other side of Merle Hay Road, the white strip-mall buildings give way to things made with dirty red and brown bricks. It becomes a land of droopy old buildings—insurance offices, payday loan centers, and nasty-looking taco places. The streets get narrower, the houses get smaller, and the potholes get deeper.

I rolled down the window, mostly because the smell of the laundry was getting to me. Outside, it was starting to smell like rain, and the sky was all shades of dark gray, midnight blue, and even a weird shade of green that matched the snot stain on my shirt.

A storm was coming, all right.

✳ Nine ✳

The inside of Mid-Iowa Lanes smelled like cigarettes and shellac, and the walls were covered with
paintings of guys with mustaches holding bowling balls.
Everything in the place was a shade of brown, orange, or
yellow, except for the glowing pink and blue neon lights
that were set up here and there. There was a bar where
people were drinking, even though it was barely four
o'clock. Speakers in the ceiling were blasting "Don't Stop
Believing" way too loudly.

"I never realized how *dirty* this place looked," I said.

"Beautiful, isn't it?" asked Emma as we stepped inside.
"A place unsullied by the present standards of design."

"Or cleanliness," I said.

"They haven't even changed the music since about
1989," said Tim reverently. "Or the posters." Sure

enough, there was a faded poster for the 1989 Chicago Cubs on the wall by the bar.

"That's the beauty of a bowling alley," said Emma. "There's nothing classy, modern, or sterile about these places. Space-age gothic on the outside, '70s leather-bar chic on the inside. And wait til you see the bowling alley skanks who hang out in the arcade!"

Tim started singing a song about bowling alley skanks to the tune of "Don't Stop Believing."

"And we mean 'skanks' in the nicest possible way," said Emma. "They're good kids."

We started walking down along the area between the bar and the lanes themselves, and I looked around at the people. There were a whole bunch of guys in ugly shirts bowling. Most of them looked sort of grimy, even from a distance. There were a lot of comb-overs in evidence.

I wondered why none of these men were at work. It wasn't like there could possibly be that many professional bowlers in Des Moines.

Besides the actual bowlers, there were a handful of people who looked like they were just hanging around. A few guys in tattered overcoats sat by the bar. Five or six old black guys were hanging by the pool tables, laughing and joking around.

Everyone there looked sort of grotesque, like they were covered in a thin layer of cigarette smoke or something, as though Megamart was selling bottled cigarette smoke as a gel and everyone had smeared themselves with it because they weren't allowed to smoke in public anymore. Maybe they'd hung around the bowling alley so much that the weird smell got into their skin and was never going to go away.

It was just a bowling alley, but I'm not sure I'd ever seen anything so scary in my life. This was not the sort of crowd I was used to traveling among without being surrounded by Lisa and her friends.

There was no sign of Norman or the Fellowship anywhere.

"They must not be here yet," I said.

"Or they left already," said Tim.

"No chance," I said. "FCA bowling usually goes on for a couple of hours. They must have had Bible study first or something."

"We can wait around, then," said Emma. "Let's go have something to drink."

We walked up toward the bar, at which sat two old men in overcoats (who looked like they might be flashers or something) and a girl about our age. She was wearing an old-fashioned dress and a flapper hat, like the kind they used to wear in the 1920s, and a long string of pearls.

Emma turned to her. "Hey, Moira!" she said.

The girl in the flapper dress—Moira—looked up. "Emma!" she said. "Have a seat."

The three of us sat down at the counter, with me next to Moira, and Tim ordered three cups of coffee. I noticed a pack of old-fashioned Clove gum sitting on the bar next to Moira's coffee cup.

"Debbie," said Emma, "This is Moira Bernstein. She goes to Roosevelt."

"Hi," I said. "Cool outfit."

Moira smiled. "Thanks!" she said, in a weird, New York sort of accent. "But it's not Bernstein anymore. I'm changing it to St. Vincent Millay."

"Moira's, like, a time traveler," Emma told me.

"I'm a *practical* time traveler," said Moira, grinning. "I'm not from the past or the future or anything, but I prefer to ignore the fact that it's the twenty-first century as much as I can. People had so much more style in the old days."

"She comes to this bowling alley because it's so retro, compared to most of town," said Emma.

"And not *fake* retro, like those 1950s diners," said Moira. "It's genuinely old-fashioned. It feels like I'm closer to the days when things were black and white when I'm in here. It's not a 1920s period rush, but it's a period rush."

"Huh," I said.

"It's a Bluist parable that the whole world was in black and white until the first time the Beatles appeared on the *Ed Sullivan Show*," said Emma. "Then it all turned to color."

"I wish it had just stayed black and white," sad Moira, wistfully.

"The *Wizard of Oz* was in color," I said. "And that was way before the Beatles."

"Yeah," said Emma, "but that was just a movie, not real life!"

Moira giggled, and the guy behind the bar brought us out three cups of coffee.

"You aren't supposed to take parables literally," said Tim. "They're just stories to teach you a lesson."

"So what's the lesson?" asked Moira.

Emma thought for a second and drummed her fingers on the table. "The lesson," she said, "is that the world turning to color should have been a gift, but we've squandered it. We must use our gifts wisely."

"Good lesson," said Moira.

Emma turned to me. "So, you know a bit about us by now," she said. "We need to hear more about *you*!"

"Seriously," said Tim. "Here we are, dragging you all over town on a holy quest, and I'm not sure we even know your last name."

"Yeah," said Moira, smiling. "I don't think we've ever met."

"Well," I said, "there isn't much to tell. Ever since sixth grade, all I've done was hang out with Lisa Ashby. I joined Active Christian Teens because of her even though I'm sort of an atheist. Or agnostic, at least."

"The things one does for love," said Tim.

"Ah," said Moira. "So you don't just want her to be a friend."

I sort of nodded and stared at my coffee.

"I've basically skipped being a teenager," I went on. "I've spent every single Friday night for the last five years watching *Full House* in Lisa's bedroom."

"Featuring Kimmy Gibbler, patron saint of crazy schemes, and Uncle Jesse, patron saint of hair products," said Emma.

"And Uncle Joey," said Tim. "Patron saint of Popeye impressions."

"Joey wasn't anyone's uncle!" I said. "He was just Danny's best friend."

Then I sighed and felt like an idiot. Most people my age get upset about the rain forest or women's rights or whatever, but *my* cause was making sure people knew not to call Joey Gladstone "Uncle Joey."

Sheesh.

"Whatever," said Tim. "Joey was a total player, whatever he was. He never had a girlfriend last more than one episode."

"So I realize now that I've, like, based all of my concepts of life, and romance, and everything on a cheesy sitcom."

"That's not unusual, is it?" asked Emma.

"Probably not," I said. "But I wouldn't know what's usual and what isn't."

"I base my life on old stuff, too," said Moira. "Last year I was basing it on Jane Austen. I still go Victorian sometimes, but the popular music back then was lousy parlor songs about kids dying. By the 1920s, the music was better and the dresses weren't as bulky. And they still had style."

"And there were movies," said Tim. "Victorians didn't have those, unless you count those five-second ones of guys sneezing."

"Are you sticking with the 1920s from now on, or going someplace else next?" asked Emma.

Moira shrugged.

"Maybe I'll go for the *Mad Men* era sometime," she said. "They still had style back then, even though the world would have gone color midway through the series."

"I guess I've basically been in the *Full House* era this whole time," I said. "I never thought of it as time traveling, though."

"At least they had a toilet on *Full House*," said Tim. "On those *really* old shows, like *The Brady Bunch*, the bathrooms never had toilets."

"So, what, they all just went in the corner back then?" asked Emma. "How do practical time travelers handle stuff like that, Moira? Do you have systems in place for doing without toilets?"

Moira smiled, gracefully flicked Emma off, and turned to me.

"New topic," she said. "What *is* your last name, Debbie? Tell me what it is and I'll tell you your fortune."

"Woodlawn."

"Very elegant. You'll have a beautiful future."

"It's not pretty," I said. "It's trashy."

"How the hell is that trashy?" asked Tim.

"Think about it," I said. "A wood lawn is what you get when you're too lazy to mow anything, so you just put down wood chips instead of grass."

Emma laughed and sipped at her coffee. Moira giggled.

"That's very clever," said Moira. "I like the way you think."

"What about Spruce Lawn Drive?" asked Tim. "Like Lisa's street. That's what your name means. Not wood chips."

"Oh, wow," I said. "I never thought of that. Her street is almost exactly the same as my last name!"

This proved it. Lisa and I were meant to be. Maybe when Lisa's parents had decided to build a house on Spruce Lawn Drive, it was because it subconsciously reminded them of the last name of the person their daughter would love forever.

"It's a sign from Blue," said Moira.

I turned to her. "Are you Bluish?"

She shook her head. "Emma and Tim have told me about it, but I've never given her the five bucks."

"We understand," said Emma. "Back in the 1920s, five dollars was a lot of money."

I looked down at my coffee and dribbled in a couple of drops of cream. I barely even noticed, until I caught myself, that I was trying to dribble out Lisa's initials. I was so caught up in talking to Emma and Tim that I was getting reasonably well distracted, but Lisa was still in charge of my brain.

Tim's phone rang again and he looked down at the caller ID.

"Debt collector again!" he said.

"You should change your number," said Emma.

"I'm about ready to," said Tim as he put the phone into his pocket. "I'll be right back. Gotta pee." He got up to headed to the bathroom.

The minute he stepped out of earshot, Emma made a noise like a wounded animal and slumped her head down onto the bar, like she'd just suddenly had a heart attack and died right there at the bowling alley.

✳ Ten ✳

Are you okay?" I asked.

"Bob Nebraska," she said, suddenly sounding miserable. "I'm in huge trouble."

"What's wrong?" asked Moira.

Emma looked up at me.

"I have a confession to make," she said. "The reason Heather's chasing us isn't because of the prank, exactly. She has a huge crush on Tim."

"No kidding?" I asked.

"No one knows but me," said Emma. "That's why she made up that rumor that he's gay—so everyone else would stay away from him. And now I work my ass off to keep HER away from him. I set up his laptop so emails from her go straight to the trash, and her number comes up as 'debt collector' on his phone."

"But isn't that, like, a Bluish sin?" I asked. "Keeping her from a matter of the heart?"

"Yeah, well, I'm a sinner," said Emma. "This isn't one of those religions where the founder is perfect. Blue will judge me on Garbage Day. But I couldn't live with him being with someone who once called me a manatee. She can't have my Tim."

"Wait," I said. "Do you like Tim? Like, *like* him?"

Emma smiled, but it was a sad smile. "Only more than anything."

"Oh my God!" I said. "Does he know?"

She shook her head in an emphatic "no."

"Do you think he likes you?" I asked.

"He told me he does a couple of times," said Emma. "But he's just trying to make me feel better about myself, obviously."

"Applesauce," said Moira. I guessed that was flapper for "bullshit."

"I'll bet he likes you," I said.

"What's it matter?" asked Emma. "Look at Quinn. You don't think he'd go out with her in a minute? He said himself that she looked good. When she catches up to us, which she will, she's going ask him out and offer to do all kinds of nasty things to him. And I'll never see him again."

Emma looked almost as miserable as I must have looked in the bathroom earlier.

"I think that when he said she looked good, he was

saying that just because she put on weight didn't mean she looked bad," I said.

"Maybe, but *look* at me," said Emma. "She's a bit chubby, but I'm the size of a small SUV. You could hollow me out and park me back in Oak Meadow Mills. I'd fit right in."

"No," I said, "you look fine!"

"Anyway, we have to stay away from her as long as we can. She didn't find out about the dictionary thing today, like I said. She found out what I did."

"She found out he doesn't get her emails?" I asked. "Or calls?"

Emma nodded. "Every now and then Tim answers the phone when she calls, but he just says 'I don't owe you anything' and hangs up before she can say a word. But this morning she overheard me telling someone *else* to change someone's phone to make someone's number come up as 'debt collector' and she put two and two together."

"She must be furious," I said.

"For the longest time she hasn't come up to Tim or tried to talk to him because she thought he just ignored the calls and emails that he wasn't actually seeing. Not to mention that I was always hanging around him. Now that she knows he's never *really* blown her off, it's only a matter of time. But I want at least one more great holy quest. If you end up hooking up with Lisa, at least this will all have been for something. And if I can last the night and we have that one goal left to cross off, maybe I'll at least get to see him naked one more time."

"Maybe he only agreed to that to see *you* naked," I said.

"Ha," said Emma. "We *do* end up getting naked in quite a few holy quests. But we never, like, touch or kiss or anything."

"Did you really sleep with a lot of guys before?" I asked. "Or is that all just an excuse to hang out with Tim?"

"It's about half true," said Emma. "It was only a handful of guys. Not three a week or anything. I mean, it was a problem, but not, like, an addiction, exactly. More like a bad idea."

"And the eating disorders?"

"Well, that's real," she said. "But I'm doing better now. He helps. I don't know what I'll do when it's just me and Bluddha." Then she laughed and said, "Poor Tim. He has two complete lunatics coming up with ridiculous schemes to keep other people away from him."

"Damn," said Moira. "What a mess." She made "damn" sound like a real swear. Not like when people go "dayyy-um," but a slow, smoldering "damn."

"Shit, he's coming back," said Emma. "Everyone act normal."

Tim walked back up to us. "Did I miss anything?"

"Nah," I said. "Norman wasn't in the bathroom, was he?"

"Had it all to myself."

I looked around again. "I still don't see them," I said. "You think maybe they *were* already here? They would have had to blow through Bible study in a real hurry to be done by now."

"Who are you looking for?" asked Moira.

"A bunch of guys from the Fellowship of Christian Athletes."

"Is he one of those palookas in the ties?"

"Yeah!" I said. "Have you seen them?"

"There were only three of them this week, and they left about twenty minutes ago."

"Crud!" I said. "I don't suppose you know where they went?"

"No," said Moira. "But you can try the snuggle-puppies. They probably will."

"The who?" I asked.

"That's one of her old slang words," said Emma. "It's what she calls the bowling alley skanks."

"It's a good word," said Tim. "It sounds less judgmental than 'skank.'"

"Yeah," said Emma. "And the bowling alley skanks are good kids."

"I didn't know there were such things as bowling alley skanks," I said.

"On the Great Skank Totem Pole," said Emma, "the ones in the bowling alleys are a little more skanky than gym skanks, and about even with roller-skating-rink skanks. But they're not anywhere near as skanky as race-track skanks."

"Let's go talk to them," said Tim.

We got up and headed along the back end of the bowling alley, past the little bowling supply shop or whatever you call it, leaving Moira at the bar.

"So, are there skanks in every bowling alley?" I asked as we walked along.

"Probably," said Emma. "The alley is like a bar they don't have to be twenty-one to get into. They hang out here all the time, trying to get guys to buy them alcohol and cigarettes and stuff. They'll hang all over anyone and kiss anyone. They'd kiss you in a second, if you want to cross off a holy quest goal right now. They might even pay you."

"What?"

"Guys at bars pay girls to kiss all the time, but these girls sometimes pay people to kiss *them*, which is a weird variation on the custom. It may be exclusive to bowling alley skanks."

I didn't know whether to think the idea of being paid to kiss someone was terribly offensive or a good way to exploit perverts. Maybe if I'd been concerned about gay rights instead of people referring to Joey Gladstone as "Uncle Joey" all this time, I'd have a clearer opinion.

"At least one of them should know where Norman went," said Tim. "They know everything about everyone."

Emma directed us past the lanes themselves and

toward the little alcove where they'd set up a bunch of video games. Hanging around the games, sure enough, was a group of skanks—girls in skimpy clothes and enough makeup that you'd think the extra weight on their face would throw off their center of gravity. They couldn't smoke indoors, but they were all holding unlit cigarettes.

And they weren't the kind of skanks I was used to seeing around—they were *way* younger.

I started to say something, but Emma and the Apostle Tim were heading to the alcove and couldn't hear me over the music, which had gone from the disco song to some heavy metal song. I stayed behind for a second, wondering what the hell I'd just gotten myself into. I wasn't used to dealing with skanks or snugglepuppies or whatever.

But they couldn't have been more than fifteen. They couldn't hurt me. I caught up with Tim and Emma just as they were getting to the arcade.

"Ramona!" Emma greeted a girl who was wearing a halter top and earrings about the size of her whole neck.

"Emma!" said Ramona. She hugged Emma and kissed her on the cheek, then pulled back. "Holy quest?"

"You know it!" said Emma.

"You sure do a lot of holy quests that end up at the bowling alley," said Ramona.

I'd been a bit surprised to see her face, but hearing her voice was even worse. She sounded like a forty-year-old diner waitress.

"What can I say?" said Emma. "This place is like a

portal for holy energy." She turned around and put her hand on my shoulder. "This is Debbie. Debbie, this is Ramona Morale, Queen of the Bowling Alley Skanks."

"Snugglepuppies, if you please," said Ramona. "We like that better." She smiled, then reached out and shook my hand. I could've sworn it was sort of slimy.

"How can I help you guys?" she asked.

"We need to know where the Fellowship of Christian Athletes were going when they left," said Emma.

"You just missed 'em. They *usually* go from here to the king," said Ramona.

"Don the Carpet King or George the Chili King?" Tim asked.

Ramona raised an eyebrow. "Why would they go to a carpet store?"

"Hey, don't ask me what those guys do in their spare time," said Tim.

"So that's where they are?" I asked. "They went to the chili place?"

"No," said Ramona. "They *usually* going there, but they didn't. That Norman guy said he had a date so he didn't want to be farting all night."

"That's who we need," said Emma. "Norman. He has Debbie's backpack, and there are some very important documents in there. You have any info on him?"

"Sure," said Ramona. "Norman Hastings. Creepy guy who always wears a tie. I hear he gave a speech in Biology saying evolution couldn't be true because there was no such thing as a croco-duck."

"A croco-duck?" chuckled Emma. "What the hell?"

"It's a theory he got from Kirk Cameron," I said.

"Who?" asked Ramona.

"He was a teenage actor in the '80s," I said. "Now he's all grown up and making videos that are supposed to prove God exists."

"What does a croco-duck have to do with anything?" Emma asked.

I shrugged. "He says that if evolution was true, there should be these half duck, half crocodile mutants out running around or something. I wasn't really paying attention."

Kirk's sister, Candace Cameron, played D. J. on *Full House*. If she wasn't all grown up and totally Jesused-out now, too, I'm not sure Lisa would have been so enthusiastic about that show. Her parents might not even have let her watch it when she was younger. I mean, it *was* about three guys living together in San Francisco, the gay capital of the world. And I swear to God that Uncle Jesse gets spanked by a chimpanzee in one episode.

"You're an Active Christian Teen?" asked Ramona.

"She just joined because of a girl," Emma said. "The one Norman's dating now."

"Lisa Ashby?" asked Ramona. She really *did* have all the information about everyone.

I nodded. Seriously, the way everyone was all casual about this just astounded me.

"Bummer," said Ramona. "But I don't blame you. Ashby's a hottie. She's funny, too."

"She's hilarious," I said.

"Anyway," said Emma, "do you know where Norman went, if he didn't go to George the Chili King?"

"No," said Ramona, "but I can find out, if you want."

"Please," said Emma.

"I'm on it."

She pulled our her phone and started typing out texts and making very short phone calls. She'd say, "I need Hastings," wait half a second, then hang up.

"What's she doing?" I asked Emma.

"Calling all of the other skanks," said Emma.

Ramona looked up and said "Snugglepuppies," then went back to working her phone.

"Having an in with the local snugglepuppies is about the next best thing to having flying monkeys acting as spies," said Emma.

Ramona must have gotten ahold of someone who knew something, because the conversation with one person got beyond the first line.

"Did she talk to you?" she asked. Then, "What did you tell her?" and "Did anyone else talk to her?" Then she hung up without saying "thanks" or "good-bye" or anything. I guessed that the bowling alley skank network dispensed with those sort of manners when there was an emergency.

All of a sudden, Ramona put her phone into her purse.

"Got him," she said.

"You found out where he went?" Emma asked.

"Sure," said Ramona. "Do you guys have seven bucks in quarters?"

"In quarters?" I asked.

"For the cigarette machine," Ramona said. "They won't give change to minors here."

"You don't just *take* information like this from one of these girls," Emma explained. "You have to trade something for it. It's only polite."

I pulled Emma and Tim aside for a second.

"I'm not buying her cigarettes," I said. "She already sounds like someone's grandma."

"Don't worry, it's a moot point," said Emma. "All we have is five bucks and we owe four-fifty of it to the bar for the coffee."

"What else can we give her?" I asked.

"Well," said Emma, "there was that one time…"

"No way!" said Tim. "Not doing that one again!"

"What?" I asked.

"One time she gave us the name of a good hot dog joint in exchange for Tim kissing her for sixty seconds," said Emma.

"She tasted like a chimney," said Tim. "And she said I was a lousy kisser!"

Ramona walked up and tapped Emma on the shoulder. "You guys don't have seven bucks, do you?" she asked.

"No," said Emma. "Sorry. Can you just kiss Tim again?"

Tim made a nasty face and Emma fixed him with a dirty look.

"I don't need to kiss Clammy Lips again," said Ramona with a smirk. "Her." And she pointed at me.

"Me?" I asked, as I felt all the blood draining from my face once again.

Ramona smiled and nodded. "Thirty seconds. Or fifteen with tongue."

It was all I could do to keep from puking. I turned around and started to run away from the arcade alcove, thinking I could probably start walking and end up at the theater by 7:00 easily, as long as I didn't mind the chance of getting stuck in a thunderstorm, but Emma caught up with me.

"No way!" I said. "I know it's one of your holy quest goals, but I'm not kissing her!"

"No one's asking you to," said Emma. "We'd never ask you to do something you didn't want to on a holy quest. We'll think of something else, okay? Give her five minutes, and she'll lower the price."

Emma called back over her shoulder that we'd think it over, and she, Tim, and I walked over to the bar and sat back down with Moira.

This was one messed-up holy quest. I mean, it

couldn't be good to have Tim at a bar if he was supposed to be staying away from liquor. And if Emma was really trying to overcome nympho tendencies, surrounding herself with bowling alley skanks couldn't possibly be wise.

But I guess I knew that she wasn't *really* a nympho.

"No luck?" asked Moira.

I shook my head.

"Ramona found out where he went," said Emma, "but she wants to kiss Debbie before she'll give us the address."

"Can't she just *tell* us?" I asked. "As a favor?"

"She will if we wait around long enough," said Emma. "She's not that big of a bitch. But information about guys is the one thing she has of value. She feels like she has to trade it for something else of value."

"But…why does she want to kiss *me?*" I asked.

Emma, Tim, and Moira laughed.

"Duh!" said Emma. "Because you're the hottest girl here!"

I snorted. "No way."

"With the possible exception of me," said Moira.

"Look at those girls," said Emma, pointing over at the skanks. "They all dress in skimpy clothes, but they're not that attractive. The only people they ever really get to kiss is each other and some of the grubby bowling alley pedophiles. Any of them would love to get to kiss a *cute* girl for once."

"Plus, you've got that innocent thing going for you,"

said Tim. "They don't run across girls like that very often in this world."

"How long will it take to wear her down, do you think?" I asked.

"Not long," said Emma. "She has a good heart, deep down. She'll decide to be nice. Give it ten, twenty minutes tops."

Too long. Every extra second was too much.

"Think I can talk her down to just, like, a quick peck on the cheek?" I asked. "Or even a peck on the lips?"

She was about the last person I wanted my first kiss to be with, but sometimes you have to make sacrifices.

"I'm sure we can bargain with her," said Emma. "But are you sure you want to do that?"

"No," I said. "But I'm sure I want my backpack back."

I was just about to force myself off of my barstool when Emma shouted "Duck!"

Tim and Emma immediately jumped off their stools and ducked down on the floor. I sat there for a split second before deciding I'd better follow.

"What's going on?" I asked, as I crouched down on the dirty, dirty ground.

"Heather Quinn just came in!" said Emma. "One of the other snugglepuppies must have known she was looking for us and tipped her off that we were here! We've got to get out of here FAST."

"But I need to know where Norman went!" I said.

"I'll take care of it," said Emma. "Follow me!"

She got up and ran like hell back to the arcade alcove, and Tim and I followed close behind. I snuck a glance back to see that Heather was casually strolling through the alley, glancing around like she was looking for someone. Tim, obviously.

Back in the alcove, Emma grabbed Ramona by the shoulders.

"We've got to get out of here fast," said Emma. "Can you *please* tell us where they went?"

Ramona paused just a second, then Emma grabbed her by the back of the head and kissed her—hard—on the mouth. With tongue. And groping. Ramona looked totally shocked, but she couldn't have possibly been more surprised than I was at that moment.

After a couple of seconds, Emma let Ramona go and said, "Is that enough, or do you want to grab my ass?"

Ramona sounded stunned. "Church," she said. "They were heading to Norman's church."

Emma looked Ramona in the eye. "Swear to me that you won't tell Quinn where we're going!"

Ramona paused. If you ask me, she was still too surprised to say anything.

Emma kissed her again, a bit softer. "Swear it?"

Ramona nodded.

"Good!" said Emma.

And she grabbed me by the hand and tugged. We ran like hell, holding hands, with Tim right behind us, out of a side exit next to a huge case full of bowling trophies.

"Keep running!" Emma shouted. We ran all the way to her car, and Emma and Tim climbed into the front while I wormed my way into the back.

We were halfway out of the parking lot before I even got my door shut.

✳ Eleven ✳

No one said anything for a second because we were all too busy catching our breath. I didn't even stop to think that we'd pulled a dine-and-dash on the coffee, making me into a thief, until Tim brought it up.

"You know we didn't pay for the coffee," he said.

"Moira'll cover it," said Emma. "We can pay her back next time we see her. She knows it was an emergency."

"I can't believe you kissed Ramona like that!" I said.

Emma shrugged. "It wasn't that big of a deal. It was just like giving CPR. Only with tongue."

I couldn't believe that she *could* kiss Ramona like that and survive. You'd think she'd transfer some gunk right into her lungs or something.

"I guess you can cross off the girl-on-girl kiss goal," I said.

"No we can't," said Emma. "The goal was to have at least one of the girls be kissing a girl for the first time."

"You've kissed girls before?"

"It comes up on holy quests now and then."

Great. Even *straight* girls got more action than I did.

"Had you kissed *her* before?"

"No," said Emma. "She's kinda gross."

"Thanks for kissing her anyway," I said. "I really owe you one."

"Matter of the heart."

We cruised around, making a few more sudden bootlegger turns, before we ended up someplace deep in the heart of the near-west suburbs.

"We're probably safe for now," Tim said. "When Quinn makes it to the arcade, Ramona will probably distract her for us."

"I hope so," said Emma. "But she might be in some kind of snugglepuppy power struggle with whoever called Quinn when we got there, and that girl might jump in and tell her we left. And Quinn probably has smokes to trade for information on us."

We had driven all the way out of Des Moines proper and back into the west suburbs now. On the stereo, some guy was singing about a boy and girl who were twin high-maintenance machines. We were almost all the way through Urbandale, the first suburb to the south of Cornersville Trace, when I had another small panic attack.

"Minor problem," I said. "We didn't find out *which* church they were going to."

"I assume it's the Methodist one in Clive," said Emma. "Why?"

"Because I know Norman went there, at least in sixth grade. He probably hasn't switched."

"How do you know?"

"In middle school, she was Little Miss Fundamentalist," said Tim, with a bit of a chuckle.

"No way," I said.

Emma nodded "Someone told me that the reason I was fat had something to do with God, so I started trying to get on his good side so he'd make me thin. Then I realized that thinking I was all righteous and everything all the time was turning me into a complete asshole, and not even a skinny one, so I gave it up. I don't think I can be sent to hell for trying to be less of an asshole."

"We figure that people who pick the wrong religion can change their minds after they die and get off with a stern lecture, if they weren't too big of jerks about it," said Tim. "So if we're totally screwing this up, we'll be happy to apologize."

"The people at Lisa's church say it's too late when you die," I said.

"Most churches say that," said Tim. "But I think it's only fair to let people change their mind after they see the answer sheet. If they're not going to play fair up there, they're definitely going to get us on *something*, anyway."

"And it's definitely not fair to expect people to think a religion that makes you a dick is the right one," Emma added. Then she sang along with a line in the song on the stereo about feasting and dancing in Jerusalem.

I liked the sound of all this. Before I decided I was agnostic and didn't really believe in hell, I'd always kind of assumed I was going there. I figured that no matter what I did, I'd show up at the gates and they'd pull out a few new rules that I didn't even know about. It was just my luck. By now, I believed that when I died, I'd probably just decompose and that would be it, but obviously I'd change my mind if I found myself heading into a light.

We rolled past Hickman Avenue, the border that separates Urbandale from Clive.

"I love this town's name," said Emma. "Clive. It sounds like a disease, doesn't it?"

"Yeah," said Tim. "Like, 'Don't sleep with that girl—I hear she's got Clive!'"

"And don't even get me started on Beaverdale," said Emma.

I don't know what it was, but something about that struck me as so hilarious that I started cracking up—so hard that I was afraid I was going to pee myself.

"Nice," said Tim. "You broke Debbie."

I can't even say how weird it was feeling like I could think about that sort of thing in public—both the name and having to pee, in addition to all the stuff about Lisa.

I wasn't worried about Emma and Tim reading my mind. They didn't seem like the type who would, even if they could. But if they were, I didn't really even mind.

It was awfully liberating just to be able to think about having to pee. Even though I felt like all of the butterflies in my stomach had merged into one big mutant beast that was about to flutter right out of my skin, I also felt kind of great.

Committing crimes was sort of a rush.

"You know what?" Emma said, interrupting my reverie. "Moira was totally into you."

"What?" I said.

"Totally," Tim agreed.

"She likes girls?" I asked.

"Well, girls and guys who act like Clark Gable," said Emma. "But there aren't any of those kind of guys in town who aren't gay, so she sticks to girls."

"And you think she liked me?"

"Are you kidding?" asked Emma. "That girl was smitten. When she found out you liked girls, her face just lit up."

"She's probably thinking about you right now," said Tim.

Just as she said that, I noticed an eyelash on my fingertip.

"What's your last name, Debbie?" Emma asked, imitating Moira with a chuckle. "See? She wanted to know all about you."

"I thought she was just really interested in last names."

Tim looked back. "Who's interested in that?"

"Well, she was changing hers, she said. Maybe last names are her hobby."

It just didn't seem real to me that a girl would like me like that. And Moira was kind of cute—I liked her old fashioned outfit, and the way she giggled, and how she'd made up the kind of person she wanted to be and just, like, *become* it, even though she was born several decades too late.

I felt like I was cheating on Lisa just by thinking about it, but it was really sort of exciting to be driving along, knowing that someone was sitting around thinking about me. Me! And someone who wasn't Hairy Nate or a bowling alley skank.

"Ha!" said Tim, turning around. "You're smiling!"

"I am not," I said.

"Sure you aren't," said Tim.

"Are there a lot of practical time travelers in town?"

"Not many," said Emma. "I mean, the goths *kind* of are, and you meet a disco kid now and then. But they don't take it all as seriously as she does. She's a dedicated retro freak."

"There's a handful of Civil War reenactors," said Tim. "That's who taught Moira about getting a period rush."

"That sounds kind of nasty," I said.

"It just means the high you get when you feel like you're really back in time," said Emma. "But, yeah, everything sounds dirty in Clive."

Up in front of us, I saw the Methodist church on the corner. I'd never been inside of it—Lisa went to a different church, and hers was the only one I'd ever really been in, except for the time the youth group played a volleyball game against the Presbyterians at their church in Windsor Heights (and kicked their butts, thanks to a wicked spike from Debbie Woodlawn, thank you very much).

The church in Clive was way, way bigger than Lisa's. Like the size of a mall or something.

"Man, I hope I don't, like, turn into a pillar of salt as soon as I step back into this place," said Emma.

"Relax," said Tim. "I'm pretty sure they don't stone people to death anymore." He turned to me. "That's not one of the things you do in Active Christian Teens, is it?"

I shook my head. "Not usually, but it sounds like more of a Fellowship of Christian Athletes thing. They might be planning a stoning for spring break for all I know."

"See? Nothing to worry about," said Emma. "We'll find Norman, get the backpack, and have time left over to find something to break and some people to see naked, then hook Debbie up with Lisa once and for all. Today will be a day of Bluish miracles."

"Unless I get dumped by her once and for all," I said. "In which case, the next holy quest will be packing my stuff to move to my dad's place in Minneapolis."

"I think Lisa wants you," said Tim. "Just a hunch. You'll be getting naked with her by the end of the night."

I blushed a bit just imagining that. Lisa and I had never talked about that sort of thing—sex, nudity, etc.— out loud. About the closest we'd come to talking about sex, besides the stuff you talk about at abstinence rallies, was that one time I'd heard her say that she hated the way the word "vagina" sounded, although she didn't expand on that to say what word she preferred.

I'd never even seen her naked, in fact. She was always really discreet—hiding behind towels and stuff—when we changed into our bathing suits in the locker room at the pool.

Emma pulled into the church parking lot, and we all walked up to the front door. But the doorknob wouldn't turn.

"Fucking A," said Emma. "Why would they lock a church? Aren't they supposed to be open in case, like, a leper comes?"

"There are a couple of cars in the parking lot," said Tim. "There has to be somebody in there."

"Is one of those Norman's car?" asked Emma.

"Who knows?" I said. "I think sometimes he drives his own car and sometimes he drives new ones off his dad's lot. And I don't know what kind his is."

"Back door, then," said Emma. "Let's roll."

We walked around the church in sort of a synchro-nized fashion, sort of like we were a street gang in a musical. I was almost surprised that nobody started snapping their fingers. I guess we *were* sort of a gang—a gang of Bluists trying to invade a Christian church. Not that I was a Bluist myself, of course, but that's the team I was playing for at the moment.

We checked the cars first—they were full of textbooks that made it obvious they belonged to people from our same school. But no sign of my backpack.

And the back door to the church was locked, too.

"Shit," said Emma. "You'd think they were *trying* to keep us out of this place!" She started banging on the back door. "Hello?" she shouted. "Anyone here? Jesus?"

I was sure I heard someone inside, but no one came to the door.

"See? I told you," said Tim. "Whoever's in there is ignoring us."

"Relax," said Emma. "Blue will provide. Maybe there's an open window or something."

"You want to *sneak* in?" I asked.

"If Ramona says Norman's there, then he's probably there," said Emma. "That means the backpack's in there. Let's check the windows."

"Who opens windows when there's a storm coming in?" asked Tim. "Seriously, it looks like we're in for another Great Flood."

The sky was getting darker and darker with clouds as mean as any I'd ever seen in my life. I hadn't felt a drop yet, but the rain smell was definitely getting stronger.

"Faith, gentle apostle," Emma said. "Blue will provide."

"This is nuts," I said. "Why not just wait by the cars?"

"Because that could take hours. And if Norman's not in there, then your backpack is out there in the wild someplace. We've got to get inside and find out who's there."

Looking back, I'm still not entirely sure Emma was being totally rational. But neither was I. I *had* to know who was in there. I couldn't just sit around the parking lot hoping Norman would come outside. Not if he might be out there someplace with my backpack.

The windows around the back of the building were pretty high off the ground, and small, but not so high that you couldn't reach them or anything. Emma walked up to the first one, reached up, and pushed it, but it was shut fast. So was the second one she tried.

But not the third.

"Hallelujah!" she said, and the window opened into the building. "It's a miracle, o ye of little faith!"

"Miracle my ass," said Tim. "That window is six feet off the ground. How are you supposed to get in?"

"I *said* for thee to have faith," said Emma. "Don't make me cast thy ass into the fiery mouth of Nebraska!"

"Go smite yourself," said Tim.

We stood and stared at the window for a second.

"Problem is," said Emma, "I'm *never* fitting into that thing."

"I could, probably," said Tim. "But I don't know if

this is worth getting arrested for. There's got to be an easier way."

"Just tell them you came to get baptized or something, and even when it was locked, you were determined to get in and get saved. They'll eat it up."

I stared up at the window and thought of all the times people on *Full House* snuck into things.

One time, Danny and Joey dressed in drag to sneak into a sorority reunion.

Kimmy Gibbler snuck Stephanie and Michelle into a movie. On D. J.'s orders.

D. J. skipped school to sneak out to the mall to get some singer's autograph.

And Stephanie at least *tried* to sneak out of the house to see a ballerina when she was sick.

They all got caught, of course. Danny and Joey even ended up in jail. But in one episode, Danny snuck into a Slaughter concert with one of his one-episode-stand girlfriends, and he totally got away with it.

This could *not* be too big of a risk for me.

"I'll do it," I said.

"You sure?" asked Emma. "This is pretty advanced espionage stuff."

"It's the kind of thing I need to start doing more of," I said.

"Atta kid," said Emma. "Come on."

She tossed her own backpack on the ground, then

crouched down on all fours below the window. "Climb up," she said.

"Are you sure you won't get hurt?" I asked, walking slowly up to her.

"Relax," said Emma. "It's not like I've never had Tim jump on my back during a holy quest before. And he probably weighs way more than you do."

I very cautiously put one foot on Emma's back, then slowly raised myself up.

"Oof!" she grunted.

"You okay?" I asked.

"No problem," said Emma. "You were just kinda on my kidney. Keep going."

I lifted my second foot up, and I was standing right on her, with my head just about level with the window, which I pushed further open.

"Can you hoist yourself in?" asked Emma.

"Yeah," I said. "I think so."

I reached my arms into the window, pushed myself up, then lifted a leg off of Emma and up to the window, and rolled the rest of the way inside.

I was in. All alone, but in.

"Awesome!" I heard Emma shout. "You okay?"

"Yeah," I called back.

"Good," said Emma. "Now, go find that backpack, and we'll go find ourselves some nudity and something breakable before Lisa and Norman's date!"

I took a second to look around me—the walls were

covered with brightly colored cartoony pictures of shepherds and Roman soldiers and stuff. There were some juice cartons that had been made into little churches on a table, and a bunch of chairs that looked like they were made for five-year-olds. Obviously, I had broken into a Sunday school room.

There was no sign of the backpack there, of course, which meant that I was going to have to go explore the rest of the place.

"Nothing in this room," I called out the window. "I'll keep looking."

"All right," Emma called back. "Tim and I will head to the back door. You can unlock it from inside and let us in."

And I made my way out of the Sunday school room and started sneaking through the church.

I'd used rough language in front of a teacher, stolen a cup of coffee, and broken into a building. It was nothing they wouldn't have done on *Full House*, but I felt like I was actually starting to become a regular badass.

And as nervous as I was, it felt pretty good.

✶ Twelve ✶

I ducked into a bathroom to take a quick pee, since I couldn't wait any longer, then walked down the hall until I found the back door. It was made of glass, so I could see Emma and Tim on the other side.

Emma gave me the thumbs-up.

"Hang on," I mouthed. "I'll let you in."

I started looking around for the latch or whatever, but I couldn't find anything to unlock the door. I shrugged. Emma shrugged back.

"Is there a switch on the edge of the door?" she shouted. "Sometimes there's a switch." I could barely hear her through the thick glass—no wonder whoever was in the place hadn't heard us before.

"Go around to the front," I mouthed, waving

my arms around in case she couldn't read my lips well enough. "I'll try that one."

She must have gotten the message, because she and Tim darted around the corner, out of sight.

I was on my own.

It was spooky in there—I totally understood what Emma and Tim meant about feeling freaked out when they turned out the lights in empty spaces. I could hear the sounds of at least one person moving around and making noise somewhere in the church. Either it was haunted or there were still people in there someplace. But I didn't think I believed in ghosts.

I *did* sort of believe that dreams could mean something, though, and now I was living out the dreams I'd had about sneaking around someplace where I wasn't welcome. I had those so often that I'd even asked my mom about them, and she looked them up in some dream dictionary that she had.

"Dreams about intruding are very common," she said. "It usually means that you worry that someone knows a secret about you, or that you're trying to force yourself on someone who may not want you. But you never know. Dreams mean different things to different people."

At the time, I'd kept myself from thinking that maybe I was worried about forcing myself on Lisa, and decided that the dreams were just a natural extension of my constant worrying about people knowing what I was thinking. It made sense.

But I *was* sort of forcing myself on Lisa. I was hanging around with her, joining all the same clubs as her, pretending to like all the same things and be the same religion as her, all in the vague hope that someday she'd fall in love with me. If that wasn't forcing myself on her, I didn't know what was.

But it was all going to end tonight.

The lights were on in the hallway, and I could see that every other room nearby seemed to be Sunday school stuff, too. Some of the rooms were clearly for older kids—instead of cartoons of shepherds, the wall had posters of contemporary Christian bands, and those really graphic posters of Jesus on the cross with things like "body piercing can save your life" written in a spray paint font. There were about a million copies of that "Footprints" poster on the walls.

At the far end of the hall was the main sanctuary, or whatever the big room with the pews and the altar in it is supposed to be called. I paused and snuck a glance into it—it was weird seeing a sanctuary sitting empty. The lights were off and no candles were burning or anything. It was kind of spooky, in fact. I still felt sort of like a badass, but nervousness was overcoming me very quickly.

Then I heard a sound. A voice. A girl's voice. It was coming from down a hallway to the right of the sanctuary.

It wasn't really a voice that *said* anything; it was more like a noise than anything else, but I could tell it was human. And even though I was kind of creeped out by the empty church, I could somehow tell that it wasn't a ghost voice or anything.

Then I heard a guy's voice, too.

I walked further down the hall, toward the room where the noise was coming from, and found myself at the very end of the hall at a room marked *Coats*.

"Hello?" I called out. "Is anyone here?"

"Oh, shit," said the female voice. And this time, I recognized the voice right away. It was Angela!

So I opened the door, and there was Angela, all right. Along with a guy I didn't really recognize. They were cuddled up on the floor, with her sort of on top of him, and butt naked. Not doing it, as far as I could tell, but definitely naked.

"Debbie!" screamed Angela. She quickly rolled away from the guy and covered herself with her arms, and, in doing so, gave me a clear full frontal view of both of them. "What are you doing here?"

I probably blushed as red as a traffic light. I could feel all the blood in my face. For a second I didn't say anything, I just stared.

The guy wasn't even panicking and trying to cover himself, like people always do when someone sees them naked on TV. He was just ... there. Staring back at me like it was no big deal. I tried to look at his face, not, like, south of the border, but I ended up getting an eyeful.

After what seemed like forever, but was probably just

a couple of seconds, I shook my head and turned away, like I'd just been blinded by a really bright light.

"I'm looking for my backpack. I heard Norman was here."

"For God's sake," said Angela to the guy. "Cover yourself!"

I heard her tossing him a coat or something, and when I chanced to turn my head back in their direction, she'd covered herself in her own coat, which she was wearing like a smock. The guy was tying his jacket around his waist like it was a loincloth or something.

For a second, none of us said anything. Then I realized that I was still standing there, and turned and bolted out of the room.

At least I could cross a goal off the list.

"Debbie!" I heard Angela calling. "Wait! Come on back!"

When I turned back, they were both laughing. Angela, especially, was cracking up.

"I'm soooo sorry," I said. "I...didn't mean to..."

"Relax," said Angela, between chuckles. "It's the risk one takes when one fools around in public."

"Public?" asked the guy. "We locked the fucking door. How'd you even get in to the building?"

"Window," I said sheepishly. "I snuck in."

They both laughed, and I even managed to giggle a tiny bit myself.

"Debbie, this is Josh," said Angela, pointing at the

guy like she would have introduced anyone else. "Josh, this is Debbie Woodlawn. She's a friend of Lisa and Norman."

The guy nodded and reached out a hand for me to shake. I felt totally weird shaking it—I mean, I've shaken hundreds of guys' hands before, but even though he was covering up, and everyone's naked under their clothes, this time I was pretty much touching a naked guy. I made it a very, very quick handshake.

"So ... is Norman around here someplace?" I asked.

Angela chuckled again. "No, it's just us. We hung around after the prayer group left."

"And you just started ... you know ... ?"

Now Angela blushed a bit. "Hey," she said. "We had some time to kill, and I thought we'd locked the place!"

"So, you're trespassing *and* doing it?"

"Well, no," said Angela. "We weren't doing it, we were just fooling around. And we're not trespassing, technically, because Josh is a member here."

Josh smiled sheepishly.

"Did Norman have my backpack?" I asked.

"Yeah," said Angela. "He said he went by your house, but no one was home. I tried to call you, but your phone is in the bag."

"Do you have his number?"

"No," said Angela.

"I have it," said Josh. "Hang on."

He turned around and walked over to his pants—

showing me his naked butt in the process. Angela giggled a bit. I tried not to. This wasn't funny! I was in the middle of a crisis *and* I was being mooned! Plus, when he bent over to get the phone out of his pants, I saw way more than I wanted to.

I turned away so that I was looking at Angela, who at least had the decency to stay covered, instead. I must have been making a really goofy face, because she giggled at me again, then shrugged, as if to say "Hey, what can I say?"

"How did you find out we were here, anyway?" she asked.

"I'm on a holy quest," I said.

"See?" said Angela. "I told you to let Emma talk!"

"I still think she's sort of nuts," I said.

"She's completely insane," said Angela. "But you're obviously having a hell of a day."

"Okay," said Josh, turning around. "It's 236-6132."

"I don't have a phone on me," I said. "Can I use yours?"

Josh dialed the number and handed me the phone.

Norman picked up right away.

"Hey, Josh," he said.

"Norman!" I said. "You have no idea how badly I need to talk to you. This is Debbie. Lisa's friend. I'm on Josh's phone."

"What's up?" he asked.

"I think you have my backpack," I said.

"Yeah," he said, simply and dumbly. "I came by your house, but no one was there. I didn't want to just leave it in front of the door with the storm coming."

"Can I come meet you someplace and get it?" I asked.

"We're at the Burger Box," said Norman. "Can you come out here?"

"Okay," I said. "I'll be right there. *Don't leave!* Okay?"

"Okay."

I hung up the phone. "You don't suppose he's the kind of guy who would dig through it, do you?" I asked.

"Norman?" asked Josh. "Frankly, yeah."

That sick feeling started coming over me again just as Josh nonchalantly dropped the makeshift loincloth to put his pants on, which didn't exactly help.

I wondered if Bluists were into predestination. If they were, then Blue sure had a weird sense of humor.

"I've got to get to the Burger Box while he's still there," I said. "There's stuff in there about ... you know ... "

"Oh, God," said Angela. "Go. Seriously. Fast!"

"Thanks for the number and stuff," I said. "And nice to meet you."

"Pleasure's mine," said Josh.

"Go!" said Angela. "Quit staring and go!"

I must have blushed all over again, but there was no way Angela or Josh could see, because I turned and ran like hell back to the Sunday School room where I'd come in, shoved a table against the wall, climbed up it, and shimmied back out the window.

I ran around to the front of the church, where Emma and Tim were waiting at the front door.

"Are you okay?"

I was out of breath, but I nodded while I breathed.

"It wasn't there?" asked Tim.

I got enough of my breath back to yell a little. "They're at the Burger Box!" I shouted.

"Say no more," said Emma. "Tim, you can run better. Go get my car."

She threw her keys at him and he ran around the building. A few seconds later he drove up around to the front. We climbed in and got back on the road.

✳ Thirteen ✳

So, let me get this straight," said Emma, as Tim drove us out of Clive, through Urbandale, and back home to Cornersville Trace. "Angela and Josh were naked in the coatroom of the church?"

I nodded.

"All right, Angela!" said Emma, raising her fist in the air. "Bonus points for doing it in a holy place."

"Is the whole building holy?" asked Tim. "Or just the sanctuary? The coatroom doesn't sound like consecrated ground to me."

"It's all good," said Emma.

"Even if it's in Clive?" asked Tim. "That almost seems like cheating."

"Clive is not a dirtier town than any other, it just

sounds like it is," said Emma. She turned back to me as we pulled up to a stop sign. "Come on. How much did you see?"

"Pretty much everything," I said. "Both of them."

Emma laughed triumphantly. "Blue has provided!"

Tim took the list of holy quest goals out of the glove compartment and crossed off the one about seeing people naked. I was sort of glad to have it out of the way. The encounter was pretty awkward, but I couldn't really picture a way to cross off that goal that would have been any less awkward.

"Think about it," said Emma. "What are the sheer odds that you could have broken into any building, anywhere, seen something like that tonight, and still gotten Norman's number? You know how many places Tim and I have broken into without ever seeing anybody else naked?"

"Seriously," said Tim. "Every time there's a goal with nudity, we end up having to do it ourselves."

"So, dish!" said Emma. "How would you rate Josh?"

I shrugged. "I can only compare it to diagrams, I guess," I said. "I didn't see anything unexpected. I guess it was hairier than I would have thought."

"Yeah," said Emma. "Guys never trim their downth."

"Their what?"

"Downth," said Emma. "It's called 'downth hair' because it's 'down there.' Get it?"

Tim groaned. "She just waits for the subject to come

up so she can use that word," he said. "I think a lot of guys shave these days, actually. I would have thought guys who do it in a church would."

Emma giggled. "Did he have so much that you couldn't see his thingie?"

"Come on, Emma," said Tim. "She was probably more interested in Angela, right?"

"I don't think *interested* is quite the right word," I said. "I suppose you could say I found her more ... appealing ... but I wasn't really thinking about that stuff, I guess. I do like guys too, though."

"Noted," said Emma.

I wasn't honestly sure about that, really. In fact, I think that seeing Josh naked might have chased away any lingering bit of hetero or bisexuality that I had in me. Seeing him had felt like I was satisfying intellectual curiosity, or checking off a piece of life experience. There was nothing stirring or arousing about it. More of a "well, there's something you don't see every day" sort of thing. The idea of touching one of them, or being touched by one, did nothing for me.

I would have liked to just take the rest of the night off to think all that stuff through, but I had too much to do. I had a quest to complete that night, and it was going to need my full attention.

What Emma, Tim, and I were doing was really starting to feel like a holy quest. Not like I was walking on a ray of light or blazing a trail of glory across the cloudy

Iowa skies or whatever, but it felt like I was doing something important.

And Emma and Tim were being totally nice to me—nicer, in a lot of ways, than most of Lisa's friends had usually been. They had driven me all over three or four towns and back and hadn't come close to complaining. I felt like I'd known them for years.

We took 86th street clear through Urbandale and back into Cornersville Trace, and soon we were rolling down Cedar Avenue, back among the old familiar strip malls.

Emma's phone buzzed and she pulled it from her pocket. "Text from Ramona," she said. "Norman and company were just sighted at the Burger Box."

"*Now* she tells us," I said.

"Give her a break," said Emma. "They weren't there when we last talked to her. It's cool that she's staying involved. Especially considering we didn't really pay her the way she wanted us to."

"I'm just glad the next part of the holy quest is a food place," said Tim. "And that we still have the five bucks. I'm starving."

"Same here," said Emma.

"Me too," I said.

I *was* really hungry. I'd barely eaten any of my lunch. More of it ended up on my shirt than in my mouth.

We pulled into the Burger Box and I ran inside. Emma and Tim lagged behind, but I didn't wait for them to catch up or anything.

Mr. Ward, the gym teacher, was sitting at one of the booths with some basketball players. He gave me a look like "Guess you were faking that headache, huh?" as I ran past them, but I didn't stop to explain myself.

I found Norman sitting with Aaron Riley—also in a tie—and a couple of guys in regular T-shirts that had sayings that looked like song lyrics ironed on to them. Norman gave me that half nod that guys always give people when he saw me, and I darted right up to him.

"Hey," I said.

"Have a seat," he said. "Do you know Aaron?"

I looked over at Aaron, who was smiling at me.

"I think we've met," I said as I sat down.

Oh, God. He was planning to set me up. I hadn't been expecting this. I tried to smile a little bit, but not a sexy smile or a suggestive smile. I wasn't looking at Aaron at all; I was looking around trying to see where my backpack was.

"Norman's told me a lot about you," said Aaron.

"Like what?" I said back, a bit too quickly.

They all looked a bit surprised. I could tell they weren't expecting me to be so ... *curt*, I guess is the word. Maybe they were expecting me to be all giggly and flirty or whatever.

"Well, just that you're one of Lisa's friends," said Norman. "And a good volleyball player, from what I hear."

"I guess so," I said. I looked around the room and

saw that Emma and Tim were standing in line at the counter, but looking over at me, watching.

"My game is football," said Aaron. "Do you go to the games?"

"No," I said. Then I turned to Norman. "Do you have my backpack?"

"Oh, yeah," he said. "Here."

And he pulled it up from under the table and handed it to me. I took it from him and let out a deep breath. If no one was watching me, I would have held it and rocked it like a baby in my arms.

"Thanks," I said. "I really need this for tonight."

"Lisa said you were having some trouble with chemistry," said Norman. "Aaron's a science whiz, you know."

"I was going to be a scientist when I grew up," Aaron said. "Before I found out that they were all a bunch of secular hacks."

The rest of the people at the table nodded in agreement. I wanted very, very much to just get up and walk away from the table, but I knew I needed to keep talking to them for a bit to see if I could pick up any clues as to whether he'd seen the note.

"Chemistry isn't all that sacrilegious, is it?" I asked. "I mean, if God created everything, he made everything in the periodic table of elements."

"Good point," said Norman.

"That's true," said Aaron. "It's not so much chemistry itself as the scientific community. They're so locked into making people believe in evolution and global warming stuff. It's all totally political."

"And it's all about money," Norman added.

"No such thing as a croco-duck," I said, just to play along. It seemed simpler than arguing that there were probably plenty of Christians in the scientific community or whatever.

"Right!" Aaron smiled. "But I can still totally help you out if you need a better grade. I know how to play the game. I just chose not to play it for a living."

"Maybe," I said.

I couldn't quite put my finger on it, but there was something weird going on for sure. Norman hadn't asked me if I was okay after bursting out of lunch. He hadn't said that I seemed like I was doing better or expressed any sort of concern. Not that he was obligated to, but it would have been nice, you know?

"I think you really should let him tutor you," said Norman. "Maybe you and Aaron can double date with Lisa and me some night soon. You down for that, bro?"

"I'd be down for that," said Aaron, smiling in my general direction, like I ought to be all grateful or whatever that he would be so gallant.

1, 2, 3, 4…

Some people get into religion because they want to find peace, or hope, or whatever, but Norman and his friends were the sort who somehow found a way to use religion as an excuse to act like douchebags. I haven't read the whole Bible or anything, but I think it's mostly stuff like "Go forth and love thy neighbor, my brothers." Not "Go out and douche it up, bro."

Then again, maybe Aaron was new to the whole scene and still kind of figuring it all out. They say there's no zealot like a convert, and I ought to know—I've seen my mom get all zealous about new religions. But even if there was still a chance for Aaron to get it together, I sure as hell didn't want to be the one to guide him down the path of virtue.

"I'll think about it," I said.

"What's to think about?" asked Norman with a laugh, like I shouldn't have any say in who I went out with. "I think it might really help you out, you know." And he nodded his head in the direction of my backpack.

At first I thought he meant the Chemistry homework.

But then another thought came to mind.

He might have been saying that going out with Aaron would "straighten me out" or something like that.

"What do you mean, help me out?" I asked.

"Well...you know!" said Norman, not helping me out in the slightest.

I felt a bump against my foot, and knew without even looking that it was Aaron trying to play footsy with me.

I dug my phone out of my bag while I counted to twenty-five in my head.

"Well, I'll think about it and let you know," I said. "But I have to go eat for now, okay?"

"Cool," said Norman. "We have to take off, too. I'm picking Lisa up at Jennifer's house in a few, and I've gotta get into my normal clothes."

"Okay," I said. "Thanks for hanging onto my bag for me."

"No problem," said Norman.

And I walked over to the line as Norman, Aaron, and the other guys got up to leave. Aaron shot me a quick "You know you want me" glance.

I had so much going through my head that I felt like the thoughts might turn into solid matter and leak out of my nose. I was scared that Norman had already taken the note out. Scared that my time as Lisa's best friend was over. And, frankly, a part of me was furious at Lisa for having anything to do with guys like these.

But I'd been mad at Lisa before. Like, whenever she casually said that my mom was going to hell, which she did from time to time. I'd be saying something about whatever religion my mom was getting into, and Lisa would say, "Well, I hope she has fun with it while she's alive, cause…" Then she'd inhale and sort of laugh. The first time she did that, I'd been pissed the whole next day. But then I saw her again and she said something funny, and it all just melted away. I couldn't stay mad at her.

And maybe Norman just meant that going out with Aaron would help me with being lonely or something. He probably thought I'd stormed out of lunch because

I was upset about being single, and being with Aaron would help. That made sense.

Norman and his friends went out the door just as I joined Emma and Tim in the line to order at the counter.

"You got it!" said Emma, pointing at my backpack.

"Yeah," I said.

"Had he looked in it, do you think?" asked Tim.

"I couldn't tell," I said. "I didn't want to just ask him outright, since he had all those other creeps hanging around him. I think he might have *hinted* that he knew I like girls, but I'm probably just being paranoid."

"See if it's still in there," said Tim.

I dug around the bag until I found it. It was buried at the bottom, undisturbed.

"It's still here!" I said. "And it doesn't look like anyone touched it."

I'd never been so relieved in my life. I almost even forgot that I was just killing time until I let Lisa stomp all over my heart once and for all. At least I'd get to tell her on my own terms, not have her find out from Norman.

"Hallelujah!" said Emma.

"Mission accomplished," said Tim. "Now let's eat!"

We made it to the front of the line. It was only then that I noticed that the guy taking orders was Hairy Nate Spoelstra.

"Hi, Nate," I said.

"Hey, Deb," he said.

"You know Emma and Tim?" I asked, indicating the two of them.

"I think I've seen 'em around," said Nate.

"Yeah," said Emma.

"What's the best way to get a lot of food out of five bucks here, Nate?" Tim asked.

"Actually," said Nate, "anything you want is on me if you guys will kiss." He pointed to me and Emma.

"What?" I asked, rather indignant.

"Oh, God!" said Emma. "I've heard of guys paying girls to kiss at bars and the bowling alley, but at the Burger Box? This is a new low."

"Hey, sorr-ee," said Nate. "I wasn't trying to be offensive or anything. That Norman guy just told me Debbie was into that sort of thing."

My vision got blurry and my head began to spin.

✶ Fourteen ✶

A few minutes later, we were in a booth, the one I'd run to the second Nate mentioned that Norman told him I was into girls. I'd shut myself down for a second—sitting down, huddled up in the fetal position, in that mental place where you'd be crying except you just feel so drained there's not enough energy to cry.

When Nate said that, it was like someone was holding a vacuum cleaner up to my ear to suck everything out of my head. There wasn't much I could do anymore besides rocking back and forth.

"It doesn't mean for *sure* that he read the note," said Emma.

"What do you mean?" I asked. "He's going around telling random people that I like girls. He *must* have read it."

"Maybe he just guessed that you might be gay because you've never had a boyfriend, and started telling people."

"He *would,*" I said, remembering his gossip about Gia Van Atta. "And if he tells Lisa he thinks I like girls, she'll probably say he's nuts at first, then slowly realize it's been obvious the whole time."

I heaved myself up and leaned against the window, so at least I'd be upright.

Tim arrived with a tray piled with cheeseburgers and fries. "These are on the house," he said. "I think Nate was worried we'd tell his manager that he tried to pay you to kiss. Dig in!"

"The five dollar bill lives!" said Emma.

"I'm going to have to tell Lisa before he can," I said. "I have to. Before she goes into a theater with him, where he can tell her and make her want to go all the way to prove *she's* not like that. We've got to get to the theater."

I started to count to twenty-five, but it didn't do a thing. I needed something else to focus on.

"Are these for anyone?" I asked, as I pointed at the fries.

"Eat!" Tim commanded.

I did.

"Did Norman say anything about what time the date is?" asked Emma.

"It's what, 5:30 now?" I asked. "He said he's picking her up at Jennifer's house in a few minutes. Maybe we can catch them on the way in if we just head to the theater."

Emma nodded. I picked up a cheeseburger and held it up. "Can I have this, too?"

"EAT!" Tim ordered.

I ripped off the paper and started eating—partly because I was still starving, and partly because I knew I was going to have to get my strength up. You can't go around declaring yourself when you're low on blood sugar. I'm not diabetic or anything, but I do get all shaky if I don't eat for a long time and my blood sugar gets low. And I would be shaking enough as it was. I didn't want my guts to turn into a milk shake.

In between bites, I tried to call Lisa again, but her phone was still turned off.

"Hang on a second," said Emma. "Gotta pee."

She got up and headed for the bathroom, leaving me alone with Tim. We looked at each other for a second, sort of awkwardly.

"You wanna know a secret?" asked Tim.

"Sure," I said.

"I've never had a drink in my life," he said. "I just said that I did as an excuse to hang out with Emma."

I shook my head back and forth like I was trying to get water out of my ears. Now *that* was something else I could focus on!

"You like her?" I asked.

He nodded and blushed a bit. "She drives me insane half the time, and she needs to be in real therapy instead of just seeing the school shrink once a month, but she's incredible."

"Oh my God!" I said. "You have to tell her. She's *totally* into you!"

"Oh, I *have* told her," he said. "But she thinks I'm just trying to make her feel better about herself, and I don't think I can possibly change her mind. It's pathetic of me to keep hanging around with her, but I can't stand the thought of her sleeping with other guys just for a self-esteem boost. As long as I keep her going on this Church of Blue stuff, she keeps her pants on. And keeps eating three meals a day instead of just eating one and puking it back out."

"I know exactly what you mean," I said. "I'm kinda used to pretending to be a member of a religion for a girl."

"Oh, I'm really Bluish," said Tim. "It's a pretty awesome religion. It's part of what I love about her. Plus, I get to see her naked sometimes on holy quests."

"I think she puts nudity into the goals as an excuse to see *you*," I said.

"She probably does. The whole thing is so stupid. It's like one of those dumb movies where there are two friends that everyone knows should be together except the two of them until they figure it out in the last ten minutes. Only the problem is, we both *know* we're perfect together but she just won't *believe* I like her back. She doesn't always process information rationally. People with body issues are like that."

"So I hear," I said.

"That's part of why I gave her the blue Buddha instead of getting, like, a Yoda or something for a good luck charm. He's fat as hell, but he still seems happy. I worry that it's sacrilegious for Buddhists, but they don't seem to mind old women rubbing his belly at Chinese restaurants, so I don't think they'd mind this."

He sort of nursed a french fry for a second or two and then looked out the window.

"I'm just glad she made up a religion like Bluedaism," he went on. "Not one of those ones where you pray to the Goddess of Bulimia to keep you from eating."

"People do that?"

He inhaled and nodded. "It's fucking scary. She was never half as bad as some of those girls, really, but she could have *easily* gotten sucked into that crap."

"But instead you guys made up a religion that keeps her healthy and productive and awesome."

He smiled. "There's no one else like her."

I looked through his glasses and into his eyes. He looked miserable. And I knew just how he felt.

"You wouldn't ditch Emma for Heather Quinn, would you?" I asked.

Tim laughed. "Hell no," he said. "What would *she* want with me?"

"It could happen," I said, trying not to clue him in so much that Emma would kill me. "Girls like that fall for guys like you sometimes. Maybe she just made up the thing about you being gay to scare other girls off."

"No one's *that* crazy," said Tim. "That's like dressing up as a ghost to scare people away from the warehouse where you're counterfeiting money. It might work on TV, but not in real life."

"Everyone still thinks you're gay, right?" I asked.

Tim just shrugged. "Even if she *did* like me, she hangs out with the preppy kids. She probably goes to parties where the beats are so loud you can't talk to anyone. You'd never catch her interviewing bowlers to find one who's bowled a 300. Why the hell would I want to go out with her?"

"Well, her friends are popular, right? And she's kind of hot?"

He looked at me for a second, then started smiling. "I get it!" he said. "It's the *Full House* thing!"

"What do you mean?"

"On TV, the geeks always spend all their time trying to figure out how to be popular, right? Or how to get the head cheerleader to go out with them?"

"Sure," I said.

"In the real world, we have this thing called geek cred," said Tim. "Most of the guys who hang out down at Comics Castle or in the back of the Ice Cave wouldn't be caught dead with a cheerleader, because they'd lose geek cred. Dorks are just as into status as everyone else."

"So, none of the guys who play role-playing games would sleep with a cheerleader if the chance came up?"

"I wouldn't say that," said Tim. "Some of them could probably be talked into sleeping with one, but not all of them. And they wouldn't want to stick around to cuddle after. They wouldn't have anything to talk about. That's why geeks think places like Dragoncon are good places to get laid. It's not that the girls there are sluts, it's just that those cons are full of people they *want* to sleep with."

"So that's why you wouldn't go out with Heather?" I said. "Geek cred?"

"Partly," he said. "That and the fact that I have nothing in common with her. She'd probably want me to buy all new clothes before she could be seen with me. And I'd rather be with Emma. We bring out the best in each other."

"Complementary Sparks of Blue," I said.

"I guess," he said. "I just wish Emma would at least stop saying Heather's fat. I mean, I work my ass off trying to keep her from thinking gaining a pound is such a bad thing."

I remembered Emma scowling earlier when Tim said Heather looked good. He was just trying to make her feel better about body issues, but she thought it was proof that he liked Heather.

Like Moira said: What a mess.

"Damn," I said. I tried to make the word sound as bad as she did, but I don't think I nailed the smolder.

"Look," he said. "I'm not going to witness to you or anything, but I'm really glad you came with us tonight, and I hope you'll come on another quest over spring break. We needed something to shake things up, like a new member. We can't go on like we are forever."

Before I could reply, Emma came back from the bathroom and Tim started coughing like he was choking on his cheeseburger and pointing out the window.

Heather was walking across the parking lot, toward the door, and looking right at us through the window.

"Christ," said Emma. "Doesn't she have anything better to do?"

We quickly started gathering up all the food to get out of the place, but we weren't fast enough. Quinn stormed in through the doors and looked at Tim like he was an animal she'd been hunting.

"Where the hell did you come from?" Emma asked.

"Through the door, dumbass," said Heather. "I'm not small enough to get in through the vents. I wish I was. I know you understand all about wishing you were smaller, right?"

"Go to Nebraska," said Emma.

"Huh?" asked Heather.

Emma was acting tough, but I could see she was starting to panic. If something didn't happen fast, things were going to get ugly.

I don't think I even thought about what I was doing. I just did the first thing that popped into my head.

I grabbed a cup of Coke from the table, took off the lid, splashed it onto Heather's face, and shouted.

"Run!"

✴ Fifteen ✴

Heather was too shocked to move for a second. While she processed the fact that I'd just attacked her with a Coke, Tim grabbed the bag of food and the three of us bolted for the door. I managed to avoid looking anywhere near Hairy Nate as we ran through the glass doors and back out to the car, though I thought I saw Mr. Ward give me a disapproving glance.

"Drive!" Tim shouted. "Head into the old part of town and do some bootlegger turns!"

Emma fired up the engine and burst out of the parking lot so quickly that it was a wonder she didn't crash into six or seven cars along the way. After a block on Cedar, she made a sudden turn toward the school, then a couple more, and we ended up back at the janitor's house.

Emma pulled into the garage, put the car in park, and breathed a huge sigh of relief. It took Bluddha a while to stop bouncing around.

"I think we lost her," Emma said.

"Let's hear it for Debbie," said Tim, "whose quick thinking and deadly accuracy facilitated our miraculous escape!"

"I can't believe I did that," I said.

"You'd think that would have been one of the holy quest goals," said Tim. "Getting Heather wet and sticky." He looked down at Emma, who was slumped against the steering wheel. "You okay?"

Emma nodded slowly, then leaned back against the seat.

"That was awesome, Debbie," she said. "Thanks a million. You really saved my ass."

"*Our* ass," corrected Tim.

"I hope she doesn't, like, sue me for assault with a carbonated beverage," I said. "She probably can, can't she?"

"I wouldn't worry about it," said Tim. "You know how many times she could have sued us for assault with shaving, sour, or whipped cream?"

The door that connected the house to the garage opened, and Jim the janitor poked his head through.

Tim rolled his window down. "Hey, Jim," he said.

"Oh," said Jim. "It's you guys. Holy quest?"

"What else?" asked Tim. "We'll be out of here in a minute."

"Praise Blue," he said with a chuckle, and he went back inside.

"Is he Bluish?" I asked as he closed his door.

"No, but he's kind of amused by the whole thing," said Tim. "He keeps wanting us to make him the patron saint of something besides mopping floors."

"Danny Tanner should be the patron saint of that, anyway," I said. "If everyone else on *Full House* is the patron saint of something."

"Good call," said Tim. "Maybe Jim can be patron saint of hiding places."

Emma sat back, took a deep breath, and shook her head violently back and forth a few times, the same way I did when Tim told me he'd made up the thing about being a drunk. She seemed to have recovered from the shock a bit, but she was still upset.

"So, can we head to the theater now, please?" I asked.

Emma turned back to me.

"Norman and Lisa won't be there for a while," she said. "Can we hold off long enough to throw Quinn off our scent? The theater's not that far away from the Burger Box."

I sighed—I really didn't want any delays. But I also totally understood how badly she wanted to stay away from Quinn.

"Tell you what," I said. "Why don't we go get my car? She won't be able to track us in that, and the tank is about half full."

"And not half empty," said Tim.

"Good thinking!" said Emma. "Where do you live?

"Down on 72nd, off Venture."

"I'm on it."

She revved the engine and I reached into the bag of cheeseburgers—I was so hungry I could have eaten them all. "Anyone else want another?" I asked.

"Hell no," said Emma. "I'm never touching another one as long as I live."

"Eat!" Tim said to her. "Bluddha commands you to eat a cheeseburger."

"No," said Emma. "He can eat mine himself."

"Is this because of that crap Heather was saying?" Tim asked.

"She's right," said Emma. "She's totally right. *I'm* the one who should have my picture in the dictionary next to 'fat.'"

"I'll shove a burger down your throat if I have to," said Tim.

"You look fine, Emma," I said. "Everyone needs food."

"Maybe later," she said.

Tim let out a frustrated sigh.

I wondered what Emma's parents were like, what they made of all this. Whether they'd helped her get help when she was having trouble. Maybe they couldn't afford therapy other than the school shrink, or something. The Church of Blue was certainly better than nothing; I smelled a lot of different things in that car, but none of them were the smell of puke. So she wasn't puking up her food in there, at least.

I pointed her in the direction of my house. The houses along the road got smaller and smaller until we pulled into my neighborhood, the land of tiny houses and dirty lawns.

"This is where you live?" asked Tim. "You could walk to Sip Coffee from here!"

"I guess," I said. "I never really go there, though."

"It's the best coffee shop in Cornersville Trace," said Emma. "Way better than Wackford's. If you want a *really* good coffee, you usually have to go clear to Java Joe's or something closer to downtown, but Sip is fine for the burbs."

"There's my car," I said. "The white one."

My car was always kept in the street. So was my mom's, for that matter. We only had a single-car garage, and we used it for storage.

As we pulled up to my car, I started digging in my backpack for my keys—and couldn't find them.

"Crud," I said. "I don't think I have my keys!"

"Did you check your pockets?" asked Tim.

I patted myself down, then started to go lightheaded. I ran my hand around the seat, thinking maybe they'd fallen into Emma's car, but if they had, they'd probably already been eaten by some sort of garbage monster or something.

"I've done this before," I said. "They always fall out

of my pockets into Lisa's car. They're probably in her front seat."

"Shit," said Emma.

"Shit," I agreed.

I walked up to the front door, but it was locked, too. Half the people I know at least leave the back door unlocked, but my mom always gets all paranoid about break-ins. Like there are that many burglars in Des Moines. And like we have anything one of them might want.

"I guess I'll definitely have to talk to Lisa now, just to get my keys back," I said.

"I guess that's the bright side," said Emma. "No chickening out now."

"Let me try to call her," I said. "Just to make sure she has them, and I didn't lose them in the church or something."

I really wasn't ready to talk to Lisa, but if all I had to do was ask if she had my keys, I could handle it. I pulled out my phone and dialed her number, but it went straight to voicemail again. I hoped she wasn't, like, avoiding me because I annoyed her. I always worried that I annoyed her. That's probably where the dreams about sneaking into her house came from.

"Hey Lis," I said after the beep, trying to sound perfectly calm. "I think I left my keys in your front seat again. You know how I'd lose my butt if it weren't attached! If you could just keep them on you, maybe I'll catch up with you later, okay? Sincerely, Debbie."

I hung up.

"Do you realize you just signed your name at the end of a phone call?" asked Tim.

"What?" I asked.

"You ended with 'sincerely, Debbie,'" said Emma.

"Oh God," I blushed. "I'm always doing that."

"See? You're adorable!" said Emma. "How can she help but love you back?"

I blushed a bit more.

"Don't you have a spare key?" asked Tim.

"My mom has a set, but she's not home," I said. "And she doesn't have a cell phone. She thinks they cause brain cancer or steal her energy or something."

"So now what do we do?" asked Tim."

"I guess we're stuck with my car," said Emma. "Quinn's probably off Cedar by now. We should be safe, at least."

"So, to the theater?" asked Tim.

"Please," I said.

"No problem," said Emma. "We just need to get some gas first."

Emma drove us to a Kum and Go (which, by the way, is the most disgusting name for a gas station ever), where she put five bucks' worth of gas into the tank—the five dollar bill I had borrowed from, and given to, her had survived trips to the bowling alley and the Burger Box, but it couldn't last us forever.

From there, we headed out to Cinema 18, flat broke at last.

"Any particular parking space you want?" Emma asked. "Do any of these spots look especially holy to anyone?"

"Someplace where we have a good view of the people going in and out," I said. "So I can keep watch."

"Piece of cake."

She pulled into a parking space, and we got out and leaned against the trunk. It was always nice to get away from the smell of her car.

This was it. This was where I'd be confronting Lisa. My whole life since the beginning of middle school had all been leading me to this parking lot.

"How you feeling?" Emma asked.

"Nervous," I said.

"Blue will provide," said Emma.

I shrugged. It was hard to take advice on having faith from someone who didn't think Blue would provide for *her* if her only apostle ever had one minute alone with Heather Quinn.

The cinema was at the end of Cedar, seated behind a giant, half-filled parking lot on top of a hill. Not enough of a hill that you noticed it was an incline when you were walking up the road or anything, but from the parking lot, we had a pretty good view of the whole town and beyond. We could see the water towers from Urbandale, Clive, West Des Moines, Waukee, and a couple of others in the west. To the east, we could see the top couple of floors of the tallest buildings downtown, and the Weather Beacon. The beacon was glowing white, which meant that it was going to get colder, and flashing, which meant that it was going to rain.

Several minutes went by with no sign of Lisa and Norman.

"Someone should monitor the side entrance," said Tim. "I'll go check it out."

"Cool," said Emma. "Keep an eye out for you-know-who while you're there."

"I will," said Tim.

"And if you see her, don't wait around and throw stuff at her. Run back to me as fast as you can. Okay?"

"Sure," said Tim.

And he took off, cheeseburger in hand. The minute he was out of sight, Emma slumped down against the car and exhaled. It was sort of like those cartoons where a fat guy sucks in his gut and looks like a bodybuilder when a pretty woman is around, then the second she turns her back he exhales and turns back into a slob.

When Tim was around, Emma was confident and bubbly, most of the time. But the minute he turned his back, every bit of confidence just blew out of her, and she lay against her trunk like a deflating balloon.

"You really should eat," I said.

"Sorry," she said. "I know. And I will. I promise. I'm just not quite recovered from the Burger Box. She scared the crap out of me. That's all."

"We got away, at least."

"Yeah, but if you hadn't thrown that pop at her, he'd probably be getting naked with her right now."

"Blue provided, right?" I asked.

"Oh, forget all that crap," said Emma. "It's just some shit Tim and I made up. This is the endgame, and I'm about to lose. Now that Quinn knows the truth about why he's ignored her, she obviously isn't giving up. I'm toast. A massive piece of Texas Toast."

"You need to give Tim some more credit," I said. "He's not going to ditch you the second he gets a chance to date a popular girl. He has geek cred to worry about."

"There's no accounting for biology," said Emma. "Guys are hard-wired to look for hotter girls. And look at me. I'm a manatee with a bad dye job. I'm just lucky I never actually went out with him."

"What do you mean?"

Emma sighed. "If we were going out, he'd really be *dumping* me, not just getting a girlfriend and drifting away," she said. "It sucks to keep going on like this, but at least this way he and I can still be friends after he starts going out with her. If we'd been going out and he dumped me, I wouldn't eat a bite for a month, and I'd sleep with every pervert at the bowling alley."

I looked at her. Any idiot could see how much she needed Tim.

"And just think," she said, "how much more it would hurt you to see Lisa run off with Norman if she was actually your girlfriend, not an oblivious crush. If it was, like, a conscious betrayal."

"It couldn't hurt *that* much more than it does," I said. "Or I wouldn't have lived until detention. One more bit of hurt and I would have died in the bathroom from the sheer pain. And if we *were* going out, maybe she wouldn't be ditching me for Norman in the first place."

"Maybe," said Emma. "But you happen to be adorable, unlike me. And sane, unlike me."

"I'm not *that* sane," I said. "And Heather sure as hell isn't, either. Sane people don't say a guy is gay to keep other people away from him."

"Believe me, I've *thought* about this stuff. A lot. That Quinn girl scares the purple shit out of me. At least if Tim and I are still friends, we can still be Bluish for a while before he drifts away completely." Then she sighed and said, "I feel like I've been walking the proverbial cow from here to Dubuque."

"What proverbial cow?"

"It's from a song," said Emma. "Saying you're walking the cow is, like, a metaphor for feeling like you're carrying the weight of the world on your back. And now it's another Bluish psalm."

I didn't feel like I was carrying a cow on my back. I felt more like I was about to undergo some kind of surgery. One that I needed to get in order to stay alive, but so dangerous that there was a good chance I'd die on the table. Knowing that it would all be over soon didn't make me feel any better.

A car pulled in with guy and a girl in it that looked vaguely like Norman and Lisa, but when it got closer I saw that it was someone else. I wished I knew what kind of car Norman was driving that day.

"And you know what else?" asked Emma. "Heather's not really so bad. She's not, like, one of those evil cheerleaders in the movies or anything. She's not an idiot. She used to call me 'fat' all the time, but it's not like she was lying."

"I don't really know her that well," I said. "But she called you a manatee, and made up a rumor about Tim, didn't she? She can't be *that* nice."

"No one's perfect," said Emma. "She'd probably make a good girlfriend for Tim. She's at least *closer* to mentally stable. Easier to manage than someone like me."

"But Tim doesn't want her," I said. "He wants you. He told me so."

"He's told me that, too," said Emma. "But he's just trying to make me feel better about myself. Watch. The second he knows Heather wants to go out, he'll run. No one would pick me over her. But we need to stop talking about me so you can focus on Lisa. Take deep breaths."

"I'm trying," I said, though in reality I was grateful for something *else* to think about, even if it was how messed-up Emma's mind was.

"Have you thought about what you're going to say to her?" asked Emma.

"Not really," I said. "I guess I never really thought it would come to this."

"You should probably just be direct," said Emma. "Just come out and say that you like girls in general first, and see how she reacts. If she doesn't get too upset, tell her you like *her*, specifically."

"I probably won't even get that far," I said.

"Is she one of those ACTs kids who get all upset about people being gay?"

"Nah, she wouldn't stop being my friend over it or anything," I said. "She might stop wanting me to sleep over, but she'll be okay with it. It's Norman I'm worried about. He'll probably say she can't see me anymore."

"She wouldn't give up her best friend for a guy," said Emma.

"She might," I said. "I think that if he says to start blowing me off, she'll do it. Especially if she's decided she's spending the rest of her life with him."

"We could both end up getting dumped today," said Emma.

I sighed. "I guess so."

"Are you really going to move in with your dad in Minnesota if she says no?"

I shrugged. "I don't know. Not right away, I guess. If we both get dumped, maybe we can do another holy quest, just the two of us."

"Seriously?" asked Emma. "You want to do another one?"

"Sure," I said. "You guys have been so nice to me today."

Emma forced a weak smile. "Matter of the heart," she said. "I hope it works out for you tonight, but if it doesn't, I'm here for you."

"Thanks," I said. "I'm here for you, too. I'm not putting my bare butt on a window at the governor's mansion, though."

She laughed the tiniest laugh I think it's possible to laugh. "Don't worry," she said. "I'll handle that one. If I'm gonna be miserable, then by Blue, I'm at least gonna take the governor down with me!"

Looking back on the day, it seems almost impossible that I'd only known Emma and Tim for a few hours. I guess knowing all of someone's secrets, and having them know yours, makes it seem like you've known them for years.

And I couldn't imagine I'd ever find anyone in Minneapolis who went around thinking putting their butt against a window was holy. They probably couldn't, anyway—it gets so cold up there your cheeks might get stuck to the window if you tried it.

I checked my watch. "Damn," I said. "I thought they'd be here by now."

"You sure this is the theater they were going to?" asked Emma.

"I assumed so," I said. "It's where we always go when we go to movies."

"Let me get Ramona on it," said Emma. "Norman might have taken her someplace where there aren't as many people in the theater."

"Oh, damn," I said. "I didn't even think about that."

Then I said "damn" again. I needed the practice.

Emma pulled out her phone and called Ramona.

"Which theater was Norman taking Lisa to?" she asked, without even saying "Hello." She didn't say anything else before hanging up.

"Shouldn't take her long," she said.

"I hope not," I said.

A minute later her phone rang again, and she picked up.

"You got him?" she asked. Then she paused and said "That dick! Thanks, hon," and hung up.

"Where are they?" I asked.

"They're heading to the theater at Southhaven Mall," Emma said.

"Clear the hell out by the airport?" I asked. "We'll never catch them before the movie starts!"

"Not to mention that my car isn't going to get us there and back on five bucks' worth of gas," said Emma. "We'd end up stranded on the East Side."

He was going to get her into the theater. There was no way of stopping them now.

I felt myself going dizzy again and felt tears welling up inside of me. My chest tightened up and my breath got short. I tried to count in my head, but only got to six before I forgot what number was next.

I *was* walking the proverbial cow. And it was crushing me.

Finally, I got enough control of my brain to stand up straight. I looked at the view of the town from the parking lot, and screamed out the F word as loudly as I could.

"FFFUUUUUUCCCCCKKKKK!"

I don't know if I had ever said the word out loud—at least not since I'd started hanging out with Lisa. I barely said it in my head.

Then I looked out at the water towers in the distance to the west and launched the F-bomb at those, too.

And then I screamed it straight out in front of us, at the whole of Cornersville Trace.

And then I turned toward what we could see of the roofs of the buildings of downtown Des Moines, and the Weather Beacon, and screamed the F-word so loudly I actually hurt myself. A couple of people walking by gave me dirty looks. I ignored them, shook my hair around, and shouted it straight up in the air.

Once I had yelled the F-word in every direction, I stomped my feet and swore at the ground a few times.

I didn't feel any better, but my chest was looser and breathing got easier. I wasn't panicking. I was pissed as hell, but not panicking.

Tim came up, having heard the noise, I guess, as I shouted it out one last time for good measure.

"You okay?" he asked.

"She just verbally fucked the entire metro area," said Emma. "It was pretty awesome."

"Why the hell would they go clear the hell out there?" I asked. "No one goes to fucking Southhaven anymore!"

"It's an old trick for guys who want some privacy with a girl someplace besides in a car," Emma explained. "Pick the least popular movie of the week at an uncrowded theater. They might have the whole place to themselves, if they're lucky."

"Oh, shit," I said.

I wished I could actually use the bowling alley skanks as flying monkeys. I could have them swoop in around Norman and Lisa, grab Norman, and carry him away to be a prisoner in a castle someplace.

"Okay, deep breaths," said Emma. "We're not out of the game yet. We just need some cash or your keys. You have any idea where your mom might be?"

"Yeah," I said. "She's probably at that hippie store by Sip. She's there most Fridays."

"Earthways!" said Emma.

"You know it?" I asked.

"Of course," said Emma. "We stock up on supplies there now and then."

We got back into her car and started driving toward Venture Street.

I wasn't quite in panic attack mode anymore since my potty mouth outburst, but I was still nervous. I get nervous any time I might have to see my mom. When I'm at home, I avoid her as much as I can. The thought of having to ask her for something—even something as simple as a spare key to *my* car—is enough to give me diarrhea.

There are some nights when you just *can't* get diarrhea. And this was one of those.

And all of this was just so I could put my whole life on the line in front of a girl I didn't have a snowball's chance in Nebraska with.

And telling Lisa I loved her clearly wasn't all I had to do. Any idiot could see there was another holy quest that needed to happen as soon as possible: the one to bring Emma and Tim together. No matter what happened, I sure as hell couldn't move to Minneapolis until that was done, at least.

It was a matter of the heart.

✴ Sixteen ✴

The closer to the "old downtown" part of Corners-ville Trace we got, the more nervous I got. There was just so much to do. The punk rock song on Emma's stereo, the latest holy quest playlist selection, didn't help much either. It just made everything seem more frantic.

"Breathe deeply," said Emma. "Try to relax."

"I can't," I said. "I really wanted to talk to Lisa *before* the date happened. Especially if he's going to try to ... do stuff."

"Maybe it just won't feel right," said Emma. "Maybe his hand'll go up her shirt and she'll think it feels good in a strictly physical sense, but something just isn't right. Something's just missing. And she'll realize she wishes Norman were you."

"That was my original plan," I said. "That she'd storm out when he tried to feel her up, and I'd be there to rescue her. But that was before I found the condoms."

"All the more reason, in the long run," said Emma. "If she's *planning* to let him feel her up, she probably won't ditch him to go be with you before the date. She'll at least want to go do her experimenting first. But she *might* end up freaking out when he actually touches her, no matter what she's planned on. And that's where you come in."

I wished she could be this positive about Tim.

"I don't suppose you've made up any good Bluish relaxation techniques?" I asked. "Or any tricks to build up courage?"

"Well," said Emma, "the best thing for relaxing is meditation. But I don't think we can teach you transcendental meditation in five minutes."

"Like you even know how to do it," said Tim.

"Well, no," said Emma. "You have to pay, like, two grand to learn that stuff."

"What's transcendental meditation?" I asked.

"It's this meditation technique the Beatles went to India to learn," said Tim. "But they all left really early on. One of them decided the Maharishi guy who ran it was full of shit."

"John," said Emma. "It was John."

"Is that the same guy who runs the Maharishi Vedic University out in Fairfield?"

"That's him," said Emma. "Or it was, before he died. There are still people who swear by Transcendental Meditation."

"Yeah," said Tim. "People gamble a fortune on it. Who's going to want to admit they threw that much money away? It's how Scientology works, too."

"That's why I keep my prices low," said Emma. "Five bucks for salvation, and it's guaranteed to offer a blissful afterlife or triple your money back."

"Even if the people go to Nebraska when they die?" I asked.

Emma shrugged. "Even those people probably end up some place near the Omaha Family Fun Center. That place rocks."

"Heh," said Tim. "Welcome to eternal damnation. Enjoy the Skee-Ball!"

"Yes!" Emma laughed. "You can get into heaven if you win enough tickets!"

"Can't you do some other kinds of meditation for free?" I asked.

"Sure," said Emma. "Meditation is just breathing and relaxing. All you do is sit up straight, breathe deeply in and out, and focus on your breaths."

"Am I supposed to say 'ommm' or something?"

"Couldn't hurt," said Emma. "But it's not, like, a requirement."

"You can shout out a few more swear words, if that'll relax you," said Tim.

I didn't want to scream anymore. Frankly, I just don't like loud noises very much, even if they're coming from me. It had stopped a major panic attack, but I preferred to calm myself down doing something quieter, if possible.

I straightened up against the car seat and tried to focus on my breathing. It didn't give me instant bliss or relaxation or whatever was supposed to happen, but it did calm me down a little, I guess. Maybe slightly more than counting to twenty-five. But I associated counting with stress so much by then that it was totally useless as anything other than a signal-jammer.

And this "covering my thoughts in case mind readers were present" shit was a habit I needed to break.

By the time we finally made it off of Cedar, I at least wasn't hyperventilating anymore.

I scooped another cheeseburger out of the Burger Box bag and nodded. "Think these are still okay to eat?"

"Go for it," said Tim.

"I already had two," I said.

"Gluttony isn't one of our seven deadly sins," said Emma. "I mean, look at me!"

Tim sighed. "You look fine," he said. "You still need to eat one, come to think of it."

She sighed and patted him on the knee. "Fine," she said. "I'll have half of one for now."

"That's a start."

She took a bite at the first stop sign, and Tim and I both breathed a sigh of relief.

We drove into the Triangle, the part of old downtown formed by Venture, 72nd, and Douglas Avenue, which is the diagonal street that forms the hypotenuse. The local hipster kids loved this area, but I didn't. It was like everything else in my neighborhood—small, cramped, and old. I liked big, spacious shopping centers with brighter lights and fresher paint.

Emma found a parking place—which was no small task, because another stupid thing about the old downtown is that none of the places have parking lots—and we walked up to Earthways, the little hippie store next to Sip Coffee.

"What do they sell in this place, anyway?" I asked. "I've never been inside it."

"Hippie stuff," said Emma. "Incense, aromatherapy oils, candles shaped like wizards."

"We buy a lot of incense to cover the smell in the car," said Tim.

"Let's pick some up, then," I said. "I'll borrow some money from my mom if she's here."

Earthways was dimly lit on the inside, and had this strong vanilla musk scent hanging in the air. There was some slow flute music playing, along with some forest sounds—chirping birds, a babbling brook, and things like that. I don't know why forest sounds relax some people so much. They always make me feel like I'm about to be eaten alive by mosquitoes.

Most of the store really was made up of tables full

of incense sticks, crystals, candles shaped like wizards, and stuff like that, and little gold Buddhas on springs. I guessed this was where they got the one that they'd painted blue.

There was also some crazy artwork on the wall, along with some stuff that I guess was the New Age equivalent of that "footprints" poster they always have at Christian bookstores. Behind the counter was a whole corkboard full of bumper stickers that said stuff like *Question Authority, Why Be Normal? and Minds Are Like Parachutes: They Have To Be Open!*

Up at the front of the room was a group of women sitting in a semicircle, cross-legged, in tight-fitting clothes like leotards and sports bras. There was a woman standing behind them, leading them in some sort of breathing exercise and raising her arms up toward the ceiling.

In the center of the group sat my mother, who was being wrapped up from the neck down in some sort of scarf while a couple of other women waved palm branches above her.

"That's her," I said. "The one who's all wrapped up."

I was about ninety percent sure that it would turn out that Emma and my mom were old friends, but Emma didn't seem to recognize her.

"What in the heck are they doing?" Emma asked.

"It's probably something to get 'centered' or whatever," I said. "Either that or they're making her into a mummy."

"I'm gonna say mummy," said Emma. "I hope they

don't yank her brain out through her nose, like they used to do in Egypt."

"Or grind her up and make her into paint," said Tim.

I walked up toward the group and said "Hey, Mom," as politely as I could.

Mom opened her eyes. "Debbie!" she said. "What are you doing here?"

"I need to borrow your spare keys and a couple of bucks," I said. "If that's okay."

The group leader stepped up toward me. "She's a bit busy at the moment," she said. "Can you give her a minute or two? This is a very complicated exercise."

"I'll be there soon, Debbie," said Mom.

I sort of wished they *would* pull her brain out through her nose and grind her into paint.

Now, don't get me wrong. I love my mom and all. I definitely wouldn't want her to spend eternity getting tortured by guys with goatees and pitchforks. But the woman drives me insane. If Emma had asked me to get wrapped up in a scarf while she waved a leaf at me, I would have walked away right there. Mom, obviously, didn't have that much sense.

Emma and I stepped away to wait for them to unwrap my mother. Obviously, until we did, she wouldn't be quite mobile enough to get me anything. We wandered down an aisle full of incense, oils, candles, and other shit that was supposed to smell good.

"What sort of smell relaxes you?" Emma whispered to me.

"I don't know," I said. "I never thought about it."

"Try this one," she said, holding a stick in front of me. "It's called 'morning rain.'"

I smelled it.

"Eh," I said. "It makes feel like I need to go make sure my car windows are rolled up."

"Noted," said Emma, putting it back. "How about this one? Nag Champa."

I took a whiff of that one—it sort of smelled like the store smelled, only without the vanilla.

"I guess that's okay," I said.

Emma smiled and picked up a few sticks.

Finally, the women in class stood up and started to stretch. They unwrapped my mom, and she got to her feet and shook her head around.

"Oh, wow!" she said. "That was wonderful!"

She hugged one of the women who had wrapped her up, then noticed me standing off to the side. I honestly think she had been so focused on being centered or whatever that she'd forgotten I was there. She seemed surprised to see me all over again.

"Debbie!" she said. "I sure didn't expect to see you here!"

"Hi," I said.

"And who're your friends?"

"This is Emma Wolf and Tim Sanders." I said. "Emma, Tim, this is my mom, Barbara."

"Do you two come here often?" my mother asked.

"From time to time," said Emma. "To stock up on supplies and stuff."

"Do you ever take any of the classes?" asked Mom.

"Not really," said Emma. "By the end of school, I've had enough of classes for one day."

"Oh, but these are so much better than school classes!" said Mom. "You can let chemists take care of the chemistry for you, but you have to take care of your own chakras, you know."

"Totally," said Emma.

I made a mental note of that for when I had to get my chemistry progress report signed.

"I've always wanted Debbie to take some classes here," said Mom. "I've always thought that she had some innate psychic ability that she just needs to develop. But she doesn't seem interested, and I try never to interfere with spiritual paths."

I decided that I had to keep talking, and not let Emma get a word in edgewise. In spite of my own tendency to shirk off anything that smelled like religion, I really was sort of getting a kick out of the whole Church of Blue thing. It was a neat way of looking at the world. But if Emma mentioned it to my mom, Mom might want to join up. If I was going to start doing holy quests with Emma, I wanted it to be *my* thing. Not another one of hers.

"I was actually thinking about learning transcendental meditation," I lied.

"You know," said Mom, "I've never tried that, because it costs so much, but maybe we can get a mother-daughter group rate. I know that there's a retreat this summer in Fairfield. We can go together!"

"Sure," I said.

"Emma, what's your path?" asked Mom.

"Mom, that's not polite!" I hissed. But Emma ignored me.

"I forge my own," said Emma, confidently.

"Those can be the best paths of all, can't they?" said Mom, as my chest began to tighten. "But you should really have some sort of spiritual guide for your journey. It makes the whole thing much easier. I tried to make my own a few times, and it just falls apart after a while."

I quietly breathed a sigh of relief.

"It's been smooth sailing for us so far," said Emma, defensively.

Mom looked at Emma, then reached out and put her palms on Emma's cheeks. "You have an old soul, don't you?" she asked.

"I think it's aging pretty well," said Emma.

"She got an old one because they're cheaper used," said Tim.

Mom laughed and put her hands back at her sides.

"Listen, Mom, I need to borrow my car keys from you," I said. "I left mine in Lisa's car this morning."

"Sure," said Mom. "I'll just go get my purse."

"And can I borrow some cash for incense?" I asked.

"Sure!"

Just then, the woman in the leotard running the class called out, "All right, ladies, let's reform the circle."

"Can you give me ten minutes?" asked Mom. "We have one more exercise to do, then I'll dig my purse out. I'll be off-center all weekend if I don't finish up!"

I sighed. "Whatever."

Ten minutes wouldn't kill me. The movie probably hadn't even started yet, and Norman probably wouldn't actually try anything for at least the first half hour of the movie. I mean, you have to build up to going past first base, don't you?

But I was getting more nervous with every passing minute.

Mom went back to the class area, and Emma, Tim and I started to wander around, looking at all of the New Agey stuff on the shelves. Most of it looked pretty silly to me. Having a candle shaped like a wizard would make me feel like I was some sort of stoner or something. The rune-stone things didn't seem all that sensible to me, and I've never understood why people think crystals have magic powers. They're just shiny rocks, aren't they?

But as I looked around, I thought more about the whole Church of Blue thing. I guess I should have realized it wouldn't be for Mom, since there was no old Indian guy making money off of it, like most of the other "paths" she went through.

And if it wasn't for her, that meant that it *could* be for me. I'd never really had a religion that I really felt like I was a part of before.

Going by the idea that there was a "spark" of some kind of magic inside of us all, and thinking of my trip to find my backpack, and Lisa, as a "holy quest," was sort of working, after all. I'd done things I never would have dreamed of doing before.

And I liked the idea of telling people I was Bluish. Thinking of myself as Debbie Woodlawn, the Bluist, made me feel a bit stronger, more like I had a purpose, than being Debbie Woodlawn, the weirdo who pretended to be a Methodist to pick up chicks.

Maybe I hadn't actually been agnostic or an atheist or whatever—I'd just been, like, a blank slate. I didn't want to say anything to Emma, at least not yet, but that was the first moment that I started to think of myself as Bluish.

Meanwhile, the women in the circle were making weird noises and waving their arms.

"What in the hell are they doing?" asked Tim.

"I don't know," said Emma, "but ten bucks says it's not as spiritually fulfilling as sneaking onto the top floor of 801 Grand."

"Or getting George Washington's autograph," I said.

Emma smiled. "Or how putting my bare butt on the governor's window is gonna be."

"You know the governor's apartment is actually the third floor, right?" I said. "You'd have to do some real climbing to actually get *his* window."

"Blue will provide."

Then I looked up and saw that there was this piece of art on the wall made from carved sandstone. I couldn't believe I hadn't noticed it when we first came in; the thing was absolutely gorgeous. It was mostly a bunch of squiggles and circles and lines and stuff, but I was sure that it was supposed to represent the creation of the world. I don't know how I knew that. It was just... instinct. At a casual look, the thing seemed like just a slab of sandstone with some carvings on it, but there was something else about it. Some sort of spark.

Maybe it was the same sort of thing Emma was saying the Beatles had. A Spark of Blue. And something about it had drawn me in so far that I felt like I was inside of it, a part of it. I'd never felt like that about a work of art before. Now I couldn't look away.

"What is that?" I asked. "That sandstone thing?"

"I think it's Navajo," said Emma. "Or Olmec or something. Or someone pretending to be one of those."

Tim looked at the little information card next to it. "It was made by six artisans in New Mexico. It's supposed to represent the creation of the world."

"Duh," I said.

I absolutely couldn't imagine how it could be anything other than the creation of the world. It seemed like anyone could look at it and see that.

"You ever read any of those creation myths where the creator poops the world out?" asked Tim.

"A couple," said Emma.

"Shh," I said. This was no time to talk about poop. I wanted to focus on the carving.

I don't think I could possibly say what it was about that slab of rock that sucked me in so hard, but it's like I had just taken a break from all of my senses. Maybe it was a combination of the art and all of the incense and stuff in the room, but I suddenly felt like everything in the world was different, like the world had been re-created just for me.

I could hear music that I didn't think was playing when we came in. They must have turned on the stereo in the store, but it seemed to have come out of nowhere.

Earlier that day, the world had looked different when I emerged from the bathroom into fifth period, but now I knew I'd just been peeking through a crack in a door then. And now it was suddenly wide open.

"It's beautiful," I whispered. "The people who made it must have been like the Beatles. It must have been six people who just worked together in that way that makes you bigger than the sum of your parts."

I started taking a few steps backward, so I could see the whole carving at once. I was in such a daze that I never even stopped to think that there wasn't really room to step backward in the aisle. I certainly didn't realize that there was a huge crystal ball-type thing right behind me.

I didn't even realize that I'd backed right into it and knocked it off the shelf until I heard the shattering sound.

I turned to see a whole bunch of little pieces of glass on the floor—apparently, it *had* been a crystal ball. One made out of glass, not crystal.

"Oh, shit!" I said.

"Bolt!" said Emma. And she grabbed me by the arm and started running. I was still in such a daze, mixed with the shock of hearing the crash, that at first I just stood there even as she pulled at my arm. Out of the corner of my eye, I saw that Tim was already out the door. Emma pulled so hard that I had to move to keep from being swept onto the floor.

The tug sort of brought me back to reality. I'd just broken a crystal ball, one that probably cost a fortune. Way more than I could afford, anyway.

I ran with Emma to her car, where Tim was already waiting.

"Hurry!" he shouted.

He'd opened the back door, so I dove in and landed right on a pile of laundry. I didn't even have time to buckle my seat belt before the car started rolling out of the Triangle.

✷ Seventeen ✷

I was a criminal now, for sure. I'd run out on the check at a bowling alley, broken into a locked building, witnessed an illicit sex act, assaulted someone with Coca Cola, and run away after breaking something expensive.

Also, it's illegal to ride in a car without a seat belt.

If I wanted to start hanging out with the wannabe gangsters, they'd probably have to let me in now.

Take that, *Full House* kids.

"Head back to Cedar Avenue," Tim directed. "Once we get there, they'll never track us down."

"Most of those people wouldn't even go there," said Emma.

She sped like a lunatic all the way up 72nd Street, past

De Gama Park and the school, until we were lost amid the traffic and lights and strip malls of Cedar Avenue.

It all went by in a sort of blur—I was still in a daze from the carving, and still woozy from everything else, too. I didn't snap back to my senses until Tim turned around to talk to me.

"Well," he said, "you've just had your first crash and dash."

"Is that a Bluish ritual, too?" I asked.

"No," said Emma, "not really. Because it's technically stealing, you know. And we already did some of that at the bowling alley."

"Well, there's nothing in our commandments about not stealing," said Tim.

"Of course not," said Emma. "Because not lying, stealing, or killing is just common sense."

"So, did we just sin, or what?" I asked.

"I guess so," said Emma. "I also ran out with about thirty cents' worth of incense."

"Between that and the coffee we never paid for at the bowling alley, we've got almost five dollars worth of karma to work off, in addition to whatever that crystal ball costs," said Tim. "You think we should, like, plant a tree or something?"

Emma shrugged, and Tim lit one of the incense sticks we'd stolen and set it up on the dashboard.

"We *did* complete the goal of breaking something,

though," said Tim, as he took the goal list out of the glove compartment.

"*Debbie* completed the goal," said Emma. "She's done both of them tonight. She broke an expensive thing *and* saw the naked people."

"Yeah," said Tim, as he crossed *Break something expensive* off of the list. "Way to go, Debbie!"

"I don't want to alarm anyone," I said, "but we didn't get my keys, or any money, so we're still screwed."

"It's okay," said Emma. "I think we can at least get *out* to Southhaven on what we've got, and hope that Blue will get us a ride home."

"You know how lucky we are that we got as far as we did without spending anything?" I asked. "If we hadn't gotten all that food for free, we wouldn't have anywhere *near* enough gas to get to Southhaven."

"Blue works in mysterious ways," said Emma. "And sometimes it's just doing the best it can under the circumstances. We'll find a way home. Maybe we can panhandle for gas money."

I could just imagine pouring my heart out to Lisa, then asking her if I could borrow five bucks.

"We can always turn in some of these empty pop cans," said Tim. "That'd get us some gas money."

"Shit!" said Emma. "I didn't think of that! We're sitting on a fortune in here."

If you ever look on a pop can and see *five cent deposit in IA, VT, MA, CT* or whatever on it, it means that every time you buy a can of pop here in Iowa (or in those other states), you pay an extra nickel on top of the price to make you return it to a grocery store instead of trashing it or throwing it beside the road—if you want the nickel back, that is. And Emma must have had a hundred empties in her car—five whole bucks worth, easy.

"That's perfect," I said. "Isn't there a Hy-Vee by Southhaven?"

"Yeah," said Emma. "We can turn the cans in there. We should be able to make it if we take every shortcut."

"That's a commandment, anyway," said Tim. "Detours will bring you closer to Blue."

I kept focusing on breathing, which got a lot easier now that I knew we weren't going to end up stranded on the East Side, whatever happened. At worst, we'd just have to lug the cans to the nearest grocery store. I smiled and looked out the window, enjoying the way the town looked to me now.

I remembered what Lisa and her ACTs friends said about getting saved, and how the whole world changed for you when you did. I didn't think I'd been "saved" by the Church of Blue, but having my blank slate filled in, even a little bit, *did* make everything seem different.

The nervousness was almost gone. I felt confident, suddenly, that everything would go okay that night with Lisa. I mean, even if she went nuts and got all pissed off at me and said she never wanted to see me again, I would probably survive. I wouldn't even have to move away. Blue would provide.

"Does all art hit you like that carving hit me, when you're a Bluist?"

"Not all of it," said Emma. "But when you start thinking about art as an expression of some divine spark, it does change things, you know."

"I've noticed that," said Tim. "It's like it opens a door. It makes music sound better."

"Just like turning out the lights," Emma agreed.

Everywhere I looked out the window, there was something that seemed different. The lights seemed brighter. The billboards seemed shinier to me. It was like the whole world had been asleep before, and now everything was awake. As though everything—every piece of art, every building, street, person, and insect had always had this blue light inside them, but it was just the spiritual equivalent of a bunch of blue glass with some wires inside. And now the lights were all turned on, all over the streets of Cornersville Trace.

Even Emma and Tim looked different to me now. The people we passed in the streets looked different. The dark clouds, which were now *really* dark, and so low to the ground that I felt like we could practically touch them if we had a decent trampoline, looked beautiful.

"Do a lot of people just suddenly look at a carving and then feel like the whole world has changed?" I asked.

"Not that I know of," said Emma.

"Because ever since I saw that sandstone thing ... it's like I totally understand what you're talking about. Everything in town looks different."

"Magic," said Tim.

"Or maybe it's because you fucked the whole metro area back in that parking lot," said Emma. "Things always look different after you fuck them. They don't always look better, but they look different."

Emma had gone in another circle around the town, and now we were right back into the old part of town. In fact, now we were in the *really* old part, south of Venture, cruising past the graveyard on Bartleby Way.

"Here's a shortcut," said Emma. "If we cut through the cemetery, we can skip that traffic light on Bartleby."

I started to hold my breath as she pulled through the open gates—I'd never quite outgrown that old superstition. But I didn't last long. Emma steered so slowly down the narrow path between graves that I didn't feel like it was really much of a shortcut. It was getting awfully hard to see, too. There was almost no light left, other than a pale gray streak between the tree line and the clouds, and the streetlights on the main road barely shed any light beyond the cemetery gates.

The cemetery seemed different now too, just like everything else in town.

"Do Bluists have any burial customs or anything?" I asked, as we passed a tall obelisk for someone named Olmsted.

"Well, no Bluist has ever died," said Tim. "So, for all we know, being a Bluist will make you live forever."

"Well, realistically," said Emma, "maybe we should write up a section on that. Come up with some symbols to put on the graves of Bluists or something."

"You should have it be a tradition to have a Blue tombstone," I said.

Emma nodded. "Good idea. It'd make it easier for your relatives to find your grave, too."

"We don't even have a solid afterlife concept," said Tim. "Unless you count that whole thing about Nebraska being hell."

"Well, shit," said Emma. "Don't ask *me* what happens when you die. I'm not going to go around telling people that I've got that all figured out."

"I just hope I don't show up in vast green fields someplace," said Tim. "I mean, that beats fire and brimstone, but green fields are boring, if you ask me."

"I'll take Paris," said Emma. "That'd be a good place to settle down for an afterlife."

I thought for just a second about what heaven ought to be like for me. Maybe it looked like Oak Meadow Mills. I imagined I would be in one of those big, spacious houses, in a bed with Lisa, all relaxed, looking into her brown eyes and seeing her looking back. Having her total attention. She'd brush the hair out of my face, put her hand on my hip, and then ...

BAM!

For a second I thought the *BAM* I'd heard was just a vivid thing that I'd imagined, but then Emma shouted out the F-word and the car stopped moving. It had been a real sound.

"What just happened?" I asked.

"My tire blew out," said Emma. "Of all the places to get a flat tire! Right in the middle of the fucking grave-yard!" She turned back to me. "This is part of why we stopped saying Blue was my car. No point in worshipping something that breaks every other day."

"Can they even get a tow truck out here?" said Tim. "This is a one-way road, and the truck would probably knock some of the gravestones over."

"We don't need a tow truck," said Emma. "Just a tire change. And I have a spare in the trunk."

"Great," said Tim. "We'll need a team of archaeolo-gists to find it in there. Probably some dynamite, too."

"I can find it," Emma insisted. "But I don't have a jack. Or any of those tools that you use for changing tires."

"Can you call Triple A or something?" I asked. "Like, really, really fast? We only have, like, half an hour, tops, before we need to be back on the road!"

Emma shook her head. "Triple A would take at least an hour. Probably longer by now. You guys know anyone we can call who knows how to change a tire?"

"Don't look at me," said Tim. "I don't have any other friends."

"Mother of shit," I said.

"Your public swearing is certainly coming along," said Tim.

"We should really have *Learn basic auto mechanics and get some tools* as one of the goals on the next list," said Emma.

I started sifting through my bag to see if anything would give me any ideas. But my chemistry book was certainly no help.

Then I reached into my pocket and pulled out Hairy Nate's phone number.

"Okay," I said. "You think Nate from the Burger Box can change a tire?"

Emma looked at me. "You really want to ask that guy for help?" she asked.

"No," I said. "But I really want to get to the movie theater in time to talk to Lisa before Norman outs me to her! So if I have to ask Hairy Nate for a favor, then that's what I'll do. What time is it?"

"Just about seven," said Tim.

"Perfect," I said. "He'll just be getting off work." I pulled out my phone and dialed his number.

Nate said he had the stuff to change a tire in his car, and he'd be at the cemetery in ten or fifteen minutes.

"He'll be here in a few," I said as I hung up.

"Cool," said Emma. "Just relax, smell the incense, and try to get your courage up for tonight. I'll dig out the tire."

She got out and started rooting around in her trunk, and I breathed deeply, but not too deeply. The incense smelled good, but I could still smell laundry and fast food leftovers and stuff underneath it.

I looked out of the window at the cemetery, and at the old abandoned house at the back of it that every kid in town said was haunted.

"Found it!" Emma called.

Just then there was another *BAM*, like the one when the tire blew out. But this time, it was thunder.

A single drop of water hit the windshield. A second later, the clouds let out every bit of rain they'd been saving up onto us.

The storm was here.

✦ Eighteen ✦

All of a sudden, the rain was coming down so hard I could hardly read the names on the gravestones. The water leaked right in through some holes in the roof of Emma's car, and before anyone could even say anything, we were all starting to get soaked.

"Shit!" Tim said.

"Oh, God," I said. "I'm going to be drenched when I see Lisa!"

I knew that this didn't really matter—Lisa knew what I looked like both wet and dry. But looking as good as I could when I saw her that night was pretty much the only thing I could control about the whole situation.

"Come on," said Tim. "Follow me."

He jumped out of the car and we both started running, with Emma close behind us, through the grave-yard. The ground was already getting soft from the hard rain, and I kept imagining that I'd step too hard and find myself sinking into some grave. But I kept running, all the way through the cemetery to the house at the back of it, where there was a covered porch to keep us dry.

Every kid in town knew about The House Behind the Cemetery. I guess every town has a house like it, one that every kid thinks is haunted. I was always hearing stories about jilted lovers hanging themselves there back in the days of the Revolutionary War. I'm pretty sure no one (well, except the Meskwaki Indians) lived here back then, and I didn't believe in ghosts, but I'd never imagined I'd ever run up to the porch.

I sat down and leaned back against the side of the porch while I caught my breath.

"Wow," said Tim, leaning against the house. "I don't know anyone else who ever actually came up to this house before. We should have made it a holy quest."

"I heard about some kids who did, once," said Emma. "They snuck in and found a skeleton in a wedding dress in some room upstairs."

"Bullshit," said Tim. "I always heard it was some gang's hideout. There's supposed to be a big-screen TV and a bunch of porno mags from the '80s in there."

Emma chuckled. "Yeah," she said. "I'm sure there are lots of gangs fighting for control of Cornersville Trace, Iowa."

"Well, who do *you* think is running the meth trade?" asked Tim.

"I've always heard it was really just the caretaker's house," I said. "But why would the caretaker need to live on site, anyway?"

"Actually," said Emma, "this is the oldest house in town. I did a whole report on it in ninth grade when we studied Iowa history."

"This is a part of Iowa history?" I asked.

Emma shrugged. "Well, it's old. But I didn't want to do *another* report on the Spirit Lake Massacre."

"How old is it, then?" asked Tim.

"Not *that* old, but it was built back before any other house in the old part of town was standing. Originally, the cemetery started further away from it, but then it kept expanding until it came right up to the house. No one's lived here in years."

"I still think it's haunted," said Tim. "I swear I've seen lights on inside."

"Me too," I said. Or, anyway, I was pretty sure I had.

Emma got up and took a look into the window, which was blocked by a dusty-looking curtain.

"I can't see much through the curtain," she said, "but it looks empty."

"Does the Church of Blue believe in ghosts?" I asked.

Emma shrugged. "I don't see why not," she said, "but that would be getting into the whole afterlife thing, so anything I say will just be talking out of my ass."

"As opposed to everything else you say," said Tim.

"Hey, there's a difference between making things up as you go along and just plain talking out of your ass," Emma said. "In fact, that should be the next commandment. *Thou Shalt Speaketh Not From Out of Thine Ass.*"

"Great," said Tim. "So I'm sinning every time I fart?"

Emma snickered. "I'm sure that special dispensations can be arranged."

The rain was getting even harder now; you could see it splashing around on the tops of the graves. There was thunder and lightning. I guess I should have been really scared—I mean, what's scarier than hanging around outside a supposedly haunted house in a cemetery during a thunderstorm?

But I wasn't scared. I felt ... calm. Of course it was raining! Why wouldn't it be raining? And of course there was a storm! You can't have a holy quest that routes through a cemetery without a good, crashing thunderstorm for atmosphere!

Out in front of us, in the cemetery, I saw a gravestone that looked like it said *Woodlawn* on it. For a second I wondered if maybe it was *my* grave, and that I'd died in the bathroom earlier that day of a broken heart and now I was living through one of those ghost stories where the ghost doesn't realize that she's dead. And that Emma and Tim had died, like, thirty years earlier and appeared to ease all the newly dead kids into the afterlife gradually, and at least give them some sort of made-up religion to get them out of limbo, or show them the correct religion in a way that would make sense to them so they knew all the answers to the questions they'd have to answer when they got to the gates.

Then I squinted and saw that the gravestone said "Wolcott," which made me feel a bit better.

"I also once heard that anyone who goes inside the house never comes out," said Emma. "Or they come out saying 'blue light, blue light' over and over again."

"No shit?" said Tim. "Like, you get sucked into the netherworld and tortured by ghosts in there or something?"

"I guess so," said Emma. "But I hear the netherworld is nothing but a tourist trap nowadays."

"Whatever," said Tim. "I'm finding out!"

Tim walked over to the door and turned the knob.

"Holy shit!" he said. "They don't keep it locked!"

"Detour!" Emma called out.

Tim opened the door and stepped in.

"Well," he said, "it certainly *smells* haunted."

It didn't smell haunted to me, exactly. I imagined haunted places smelling musty, or maybe like formaldehyde. But when I followed Emma and Tim inside, I just smelled beer and barf.

As we roamed through the lower level of the house, it became pretty apparent why it smelled that way. In what I guess used to be the living room, there was a beat-up couch, about a hundred empty beer cans, and, to my great surprise, the infamous big-screen TV. It was an old, boxy one, but it looked like it was in decent shape. There were stains on the walls, the floors, and the ceiling.

So, the lights didn't come on because the house was haunted. They came on because it was a party pit.

"Well," said Emma, "I think we just solved about eight mysteries in one. Kind of a letdown."

"This sucks," said Tim. "I spent my whole life thinking this place was haunted, and now I find out it's just been a place for kids to get wasted."

"And not invite us, naturally," said Emma, who sounded rather pissed off.

"You wouldn't go anyway," said Tim.

"It's the principle of the thing," said Emma.

I wandered around, looking for something mysterious. An old picture, an actual ghost. Anything. But it was just empty cans and bottles, some dirty words scribbled on the dirty walls. I wondered how many "haunted houses" were really just abandoned places where people go to drink or get stoned.

"Hmm," I said. "The stains are kind of mysterious."

"I wish that were true," said Tim. "But I'm afraid I can tell exactly which fluid was which. Gross."

Okay. The rest of the town had seemed sort of … holy and beautiful. But there was a limit to how far that whole thing of the "door opening" went, obviously. I wasn't seeing beautiful patterns in the stains.

"Well, there's money to be made while we wait," said Emma. She started gathering up the empty cans and bottles and throwing them into one of the empty grocery bags that were scattered here and there among the trash.

Through the window, I saw a car pull up behind Emma's car, and after a second Nate and a couple of girls got out. I went out onto the porch and waved, so they'd know where we were.

I half expected that one of the two girls was going to turn out to be Heather Quinn. But it wasn't.

One of them was Ramona, the snugglepuppy.

And the other was Moira, the practical time traveler.

✳ Nineteen ✳

R amona!" said Emma. "And Moira!"

"Hey, Emma," Moira called out as they ran through the rain to the porch. "You owe me $4.50 for those coffees you wiggled out on at Mid-Iowa!"

"I'll have to get you later," said Emma. "We're flat broke right now."

"I know you're good for it," said Moira.

"You three know each other?" I asked.

"Well, duh," said Ramona. "Natey's one of the best bowlers in town."

Nate smiled proudly.

"I figured you guys'd be hiding out in here," he said. "Is the TV working?"

"You've been in here before?" I asked.

"Oh, yeah," he said. "Tons of times. It's the safest place in town to drink without getting arrested. I guess some guy out in Montana just owns it for tax purposes, but he keeps the electricity running, for some reason."

"So there's no dead bride lying on a bed upstairs?" I asked.

"Nah," said Nate, stepping inside. He seemed right at home among the beer cans and puke stains. Ramona followed him, holding his hand adoringly. "I heard some shit like that when they first started breaking in, but I ain't never seen nothing spooky in here."

"There's a bed up there, though," said Ramona. "I know a couple of people who lost their virginity there."

Ew.

"And if you took a survey of all the girls in Des Moines," said Nate, "I'll bet it would turn out that half of them first got it on either here or at that grave in that cemetery by the science center that's supposed to be all enchanted and shit."

"Seriously," said Ramona. "Like, everyone I know had their first kiss in a graveyard. Or in that nook behind Earthways where you can park without anyone seeing you."

"Look," I said, "we really need the tire fixed fast. We have to get out to the movies before Lisa and Norman's movie ends."

"Well," said Hairy Nate, "I'll get started as soon as you pay up."

"We're broke," I said. I thought it was pretty tacky for

him to ask for cash up front for a favor, but I didn't have time to argue over manners and ethics.

"No cash," said Nate. "I just want to see you and you kiss." And he pointed to me and Ramona.

"What?" I asked.

"We planned the whole thing on the way," said Ramona. "The deal back at the bowling alley was a kiss from you, and all I got was one from Emma!"

"Is that such a terrible trade?" asked Emma.

Nate did a kind of half-laugh thing, and I was sure he was about to make some crack about Emma being overweight, which would have been my cue to slap him upside the head. But he didn't say anything.

I noticed Nate kind of leering at me, then looked down and noticed that, with my shirt wet, you could totally see my bra through it. I blushed and crossed my arms over my chest.

"I don't care who kisses who," said Nate. "As long as it's girl-on-girl."

"But I've already kissed Emma," said Ramona. "I want to kiss Debbie!"

"You can't make her kiss anyone," said Emma. "Isn't there something I can do? Or Tim?"

"A deal's a deal," said Ramona, smirking. "And by the way, you'd better hurry. I heard that Lisa and Jennifer were at the indoor pool in Urbandale."

"They went swimming?" I asked.

"No," said Ramona. "They were leafing through

everyone's magazines looking at the sex tips. Sounds like tonight's the night."

Lightning crashed, right on cue, and the thunder roared. The wind pounded sheets of rain into the walls.

Every time a situation had come up where I might end up kissing someone—like, say, in drama class or when I got invited to a party where there might be a spin-the-bottle game or something—all I could think about (surprise, surprise) was *Full House*. Especially the episode with D. J.'s thirteenth birthday where Becky tells her that a kiss is a very personal, private thing. Especially your *first* kiss.

But if Ramona was telling the truth, not just bluffing, Lisa really was planning to go all the way with Norman, and she hadn't even told me. She was running around town with Jennifer telling her things she wouldn't tell me! I didn't know if it was a sign that she had a big secret she was keeping from me, or if she'd been lying to me every time she'd talked about virginity, or what.

Although, now that I thought of it, she never really talked about "virginity," exactly. She mostly talked about how you were only supposed to be with one person for life. If she let Norman do anything beyond kissing, she might feel like she had to stay with him forever so it wouldn't be a sin, even if he turned out to be a horrible, abusive bastard, not just a boring jerk.

I had to get that tire replaced. No matter what it took.

I didn't want my first kiss to be with a bowling alley skank, but Ramona wasn't the only girl in the room.

I took two deep breaths and focused hard on the breathing, then walked up to Nate, Moira, and Ramona and looked the three of them over.

"Who's fixing the tire, Nate?" I asked. "You or Ramona?"

"I am," said Nate.

"And you don't care which girl I kiss, do you?"

He shook his head. "I ain't picky."

I moved forward, put my hand on the back of Moira's head, and said, "Do you mind?"

Moira looked shocked for a second, then she sort of smiled. "Be my guest," she said.

My knees buckled, but I got ahold of myself, took one more deep breath, and kissed her.

And not just a peck, either. I wanted this to *count*. I opened my mouth and kissed her like I meant it.

I didn't close my eyes, so I could see by the look in hers that she was awfully surprised, but after a second or so, she started kissing back. That was when I let her go. I mean, it felt good and all—everything I'd ever thought a kiss might feel like—but making it more than a show started to make me feel like I was cheating on Lisa or something.

"Whoa, baby!" said Ramona.

"Have mercy," Emma laughed.

Moira was grinning like a fool, and blushing a bit. I

was, too, probably. Actually, I was probably blushing a lot. But I got ahold of myself.

"Will that do?" I asked Nate.

"*Hell* yeah."

I was rather proud of myself. It would have been better if I'd eaten a mint first, instead of a bunch of cheeseburgers, but I'd done a damn good job, if I do say so myself.

And it was something the old Debbie, the one I'd symbolically flushed down the toilet that afternoon, would never, ever have done.

"I'll give you ten bucks to do that again," said Nate.

"Just fix the tire, please," I said to him.

"Done."

And he disappeared back outside.

"That was awesome!" said Emma. "They didn't teach you to do that on *Full House*, did they?"

"Just instinct," I said.

"Hallelujah!" said Emma. "And that's the last goal—you finished the whole fucking list!"

"Anything can happen on a night when we finish off a holy quest goal list," said Tim. "Anything."

"Wasn't the quest to hook Debbie up with Lisa?" asked Ramona.

"That's the main part," said Emma. "But we had a checklist of stuff to do along the way, and Debbie turned out to be a real pro."

I smiled proudly again.

"I hope you steal Lisa's ass back from Hastings," said

Ramona. "He once sort of hinted that I'd go to hell for showing so much cleavage. Like God doesn't want *this* in heaven?" She stuck out her chest proudly.

And I stood there proudly, too. I was kicking ass and taking names and sending them in with two proofs of purchase and $2.95 for shipping and handling. And it was all doing stuff I wouldn't have dreamed of doing that morning.

This was probably the feeling that my mom was going for with all of her classes and stuff. Only she'd spent years trying to get there, not to mention a hell of a lot of money that we could have used to get a nicer place or whatever. And I'd done it in a couple hours for about the price of a sandwich. Not half bad. In fact, it was the best five dollars I'd ever spent.

Ramona looked over at me. "Sure you won't kiss me? I'll split the ten from Nate with you."

I shook my head. "I cost way more than that," I said.

"Attagirl," said Emma. "But if you want to start kissing for money, I can totally be your manager. I'll get you the best rates in town."

"Nah," I said. "I'm okay doing it in an emergency, but taking money is really only a few steps up the ladder from being a prostitute, isn't it?"

"No!" said Ramona.

And I realized I'd just made a major faux pas—kissing for money was how she made a living, and I'd just sort of called her a hooker.

"It's not like I go all the way for money, you know," she said. "It's no different than when actors kiss other actors. They aren't prostitutes."

"Fair enough," I said. "But I've never been much of an actress."

"Maybe not," said Ramona, "but was that as good as it looked, Moira?"

"Certainly." Moira grinned.

I smiled. I hadn't really thought about whether it was good or not. I wasn't really thinking like that. But it definitely didn't feel *bad*.

"See?" said Ramona. "If you keep kissing people like that, you could make a killing at the bowling alley. And people at real bars pay way more, if you can get into those."

"I'll keep that in mind," I said.

I looked at Moira and sort of blushed, then turned away from her to read the graffiti on the walls, some of which was dated as far back as the late 1970s. Most of it was really obscene stuff, like drawings of genitals and names of girls who were good at various things I don't care to repeat. It was weird to think that all that stuff went on even in Des Moines. Just like it was weird to think that there were bowling alley skanks, practical time-travelers, and Bluists roaming around. This was a side of the city that you didn't see at ACTs picnics, even though I was sure some of the girls whose names were on the wall had been ACTs members.

It was weird to think there were even people like *me* in Des Moines.

In fact, the more I thought about it, the more it seemed like everyone in the world was a total weirdo. No one was *normal*, really. Maybe not even my dad.

After a few minutes, Hairy Nate came back into the house, soaking wet but smiling.

"All right," he said. "You're all set."

"Thanks!" I said. I ran up and hugged him. He hugged me back, and I felt one of his hands moving south down my spine. I pulled away before he could get to my butt.

"There's gonna be a party here in a couple of nights," said Nate. "Should be pretty wild."

"I'll keep it in mind," I said. "But we've got to go!"

"Just so you know," said Ramona, "someone in the chain is leaking information to Quinn. I don't know who yet, but it's a safe bet she'll find out you're going to the mall."

"We'll keep our eyes out," said Emma.

We hustled out the door, through the rain, and back to Emma's car. We drove out of the cemetery and headed for Euclid Avenue. As we went by, I looked out at the Wolcott gravestone that I'd thought said Woodlawn at first. It was a nice-looking stone, really. If it had been mine, it wouldn't have been the worst thing in the world.

But I wasn't dead yet.

Not even close.

✴ Twenty ✴

We cut around the highway and back through the old downtown. I had to admit, this part of Cornersville Trace looked sort of stylish and charming in the rain after dark. It still seemed a bit crowded and old for my taste, honestly, but I guess it wasn't without its charm.

"Does everyone around here really have their first kiss in a cemetery?" I asked.

"I did," said Emma. "The guy I was with actually pulled into one to make his move."

"Weird," I said.

"I think maybe the land they're on has some sort of energy, some sort of Blue," she said. "Like ley lines or something. It's why people turn them into sacred grounds to start with. They sort of pick up on it when they're first settling the town or whatever."

"That makes sense," said Tim. "I hear a lot of newer cemeteries turn out to be built on Indian burial grounds."

"That's just the kind of thing some people *would* say," said Emma. "But let's call it a Bluish belief that cemeteries are usually built in spaces that people instinctively find sacred."

"I'll add it to the notebook," said Tim. "I've got to update it, anyway, after Debbie's latest brilliant maneuver."

He pulled the list of holy quest goals out of the glove compartment and crossed off the last one.

"That's all three," he said. "Something big is going to happen tonight. Debbie, you could just about take credit for making it rain!"

The rain was coming down hard enough to drown a turkey (as my grandmother would have said), and it was falling right through the holes in the car roof. Tim held up two of Emma's shirts—one to keep him dry, and one to keep Emma dry. I tried holding up a Neighborhood Watch sign, but it didn't do much good; the drops rolled off it and onto me, so I ended up holding up a shirt too, which absorbed the water better.

The holy quest playlist selection of the moment was a pretty-sounding song by the Decemberists, a band Emma said I'd like, but the volume was low enough that I could hardly hear it over the storm outside—not to mention the drips inside the car.

"Well," said Emma, "did I tell you to trust in Blue, or didn't I? We've crossed off just about every goal on the list in one night, and we're about to go get you your girlfriend!"

"Can you turn the music up?" I asked. "I want to hear if music seems different now. Like art does."

"Of course!" she said.

Emma turned the volume up just as the Decemberists song was ending. The next song started out sounding like some sort of Christmas carol, with horns and jingle bells and stuff, but the first line the singer sang was telling someone that he may not always love her. Not exactly Christmasy. It was pretty, though.

"Who's this?" I asked.

"The Beach Boys," Emma replied.

"What?" I asked. "No way!"

"Sure," said Emma. "It's called 'God Only Knows.'"

The Beach Boys were about the only rock band I really knew much about. In the world of *Full House*, they were the biggest, most popular band on the planet. They showed up as guest stars now and then.

When the song got to the chorus I realized that I'd heard the song plenty of times over the years, on car stereos and playing quietly in the mall and stuff. I'd just never realized it was the Beach Boys. Or that it was so incredibly gorgeous.

"I didn't know the Beach Boys did songs like this," I said. "I thought it was all songs about surfing and cars and, like, sandcastles and stuff."

"Yeah," said Tim, "they were kind of secretly awesome. The guy who arranged their songs said they were teenage symphonies to God. And some guy once said the strings on this song are proof of divinity."

"It was the guy from U2," said Emma. "Either that or Elvis Costello. But if I see one more hipster on the Internet saying that their *Pet Sounds* record is better than *Abbey Road*, I'll pound them into sand and make a castle of my own."

I shut up for a minute and let the music play. It was gorgeous. Maybe it was just that Emma had turned the volume *way* up, but it sounded almost like the voices were straining to break out of the stereo and go forth into the world.

And toward the end, when each of the Beach Boys took turns singing the main chorus line, one after the other, piling harmonies on top of each other like a choir of angels who didn't know what they'd be without whoever they were singing to, I looked around the car and felt like I knew what everyone was thinking.

Tim didn't know what he'd be without Emma.

Emma didn't know what she'd be without Tim.

And I didn't know what I'd be without Lisa.

It killed me to see both Emma and Tim so miserable about each other. I was totally going to have to make sure they ran into Heather soon and got it over with. Emma might just about pass out, but Tim wouldn't ditch her. She'd see. After all they'd done for me that day, it was the least I could do.

When the song ended, Emma pushed another button without a word, and another Beach Boys song I already knew, "Wouldn't it Be Nice," came on. It hit me just as hard as the other one. All those lines about how nice it would be to be grown up and in love in a world where no one told you that you were too young or too stupid or that you shouldn't be sleeping together. It was happy and bouncy, like how I always thought of Beach Boys songs, but you could hear this wistful sadness behind it all that I'd never noticed before.

The week before, I'd taken an online survey where they asked me what my favorite color, food, and movie were and all of that. It was sort of depressing, because I barely watched any movies or anything. The whole thing felt like a wake-up call to get out more. I ended up just making up dumb answers, like I told them my favorite song was "He's Our Dad (He's Got a Really Clean Room)," the song D. J. and Stephanie pretended they were writing on the *Full House* episode where they busted a hole in Danny's bedroom wall. It was a terrible, terrible song.

Would all music sound this incredible now? Like, would even crap sound like art to me now?

Well, no. I found that out fast enough. The next song Emma played was some song that just sounded like feedback and noise. It didn't sound like art at all. The rest of the songs she played as we drove were hit or miss. But the hits sounded unbelievable; it was like I was hearing music—not just *this* music, but *music*—for the first time.

We finally made it to Southhaven Mall, soaking wet and freezing cold, with about forty-five minutes to spare before a 7:00 movie would let out. My yogurt-and-snot-stained shirt was also soaking wet now, so I fished a royal blue sweater out of the laundry pile, waved some incense over it in attempt to cover the smell, and put it on. I was still going to be a chilly, damp, and slightly stinky mess, but I could handle it.

After all, I always thought I looked sort of cute with wet hair. One time, after we went swimming in seventh grade, Lisa even told me that I did. It was just a casual thing, like "Hey, your hair looks cute like that," but I've replayed it in my head a million times.

"All right," said Emma. "Ready to do this thing?"

"Ready as I'll ever be," I said.

I reached up and rubbed Bluddha's head. I don't know if it's just because my hands were wet or because I rubbed too hard, but some of the paint came off. When I moved my hand away, there was a spark of gold on his head, peeking out from beneath the blue. That had to be a good omen.

"Let's roll," said Tim.

We dashed out of the car and ran like hell through the rain to the main entrance. I honestly couldn't remember when I'd last been at Southhaven Mall—most of the shopping I did was at the strip malls on Cedar. If I went to any mall, it was usually Jordan Creek, the one out in West Des Moines.

Inside, I saw that everybody *else* must have been shopping in Jordan Creek, too. Southhaven Mall was in bad shape. Some of the stores were shut up, and there weren't many people wandering around.

I'd expected the place to be jumping. I mean, it was Friday night, the beginning of spring break. Shouldn't even a dumpy mall like Southhaven have been packed with teenagers from the East Side? Then again, maybe the whole "hanging out at the mall" thing was just another thing from the *Full House* era that I hadn't realized was out-of-date now.

"Where is everyone?" I asked.

"Actually," said Emma, "this is fairly crowded, as this mall goes. People aren't as into strip malls when there's a storm going on."

"Weird," I said.

I felt almost like I was wandering through some European village after World War II that was full of bombed-out houses, closed storefronts, and rubble. One place that was a toy store when I was a kid was a lingerie and adult novelties shop now. Even a lot of the stores that were left seemed weird—there was a dance studio, a pawn shop, something called "Vampire Connection," and a church, even. In the mall! Who goes to church in the mall?

We started walking down the main corridor of the mall, past this giant statue of a naked guy (complete with penis) riding a tricycle. He had enormous angel wings on his back that looked almost like they were made of bronzed flames. I couldn't help but stare at the thing as we walked by. There used to be another one just like it at Monk Hill, the mall back in Cornersville Trace (or maybe this was the same one, and they'd just moved it since the last time I was there), but I guess I'd never noticed how weird it was.

The whole world really did seem different now. How had I not noticed before that a big naked angel on a trike is weird?

And as we passed it, I saw that someone had written the words *Saint Merle the Naked* in black marker on the brick base. I had a pretty good idea who did that. Emma had probably decided that the statue was a Bluish figurehead.

I nodded my head toward it and thought, "Saint Merle, if you can throw me any help tonight, I could use it!" I was also silently praying to every other deity I could think of, just to hedge my bets, as I imagined Saint Merle swooping in from the sky on his tricycle to bless me.

But as we approached the theater, my first instinct was to chicken out.

"I don't know about this," I said. "The mall might close before the movie ends. They'll probably throw us out into the rain."

"There's a canopy we can stand under," said Emma.

"Still," I said. "Maybe I should just find her tomorrow."

"That might be too late," said Emma. "She might sleep with him tonight."

I cringed. "Well, the first time is always bad, isn't it?" I asked. "Maybe I can take advantage of her disappointment in the morning."

Emma gave my hand a squeeze.

"Be brave," she said. "You can do this. You were saying that if she let him go much past first, she'd want to stay with him forever just on general principle, right?"

I nodded.

"They won't do it *in* the theater, probably," she went on. "That wouldn't be comfortable. But the car, later, is a possibility. He could drive her into a graveyard or the nook behind Earthways, if it's not already taken. So you have to talk to her tonight. Tomorrow might be too late."

"In the meantime, we have a minor problem," said Tim. "Look!"

Heather Quinn was walking into the mall, just as Ramona had predicted.

"Oh, shit," Emma said. "She must have picked something up from a snugglepuppy after Ramona made those calls."

Personally, I was glad to see her. I wasn't quite ready to face my own fears, but I was ready to help Emma face hers. I'd saved her ass a couple of times that night, and now it was time to save her heart.

"You guys run," I said. "I'll get rid of her. Meet me at the record store in ten minutes."

Emma nodded, and she and Tim ran like hell. As soon as they were safely away, I turned toward Heather.

"Hey, Heather," I called out, and she came up to me.

"Where are they?" she demanded.

"Calm down," I said. "I'm on your side. They're meeting me at the record store. Come there with me, and I'll block the exit after they come in."

Heather thought for a second, then nodded.

"Okay," she said. "You're all right, Woodlawn."

"Sorry about the Coke earlier," I said. "They kinda gave me no choice."

"Whatever," she said. "They would."

And we wandered down the walkway, past St. Merle the Naked and toward the record store.

"I can't believe Tim has been hanging out with that girl all this time," Heather whined. "What the heck does he see in that manatee?"

"Beats me," I said, even though it killed me. "I guess he thinks she's really creative and spontaneous."

"*I'm* creative!" Heather said. "And does she even know how lucky a geekburger like Tim would be to go out with someone like me? It took me a long time to admit to myself that I even liked him. He's so not the kind of guy I'm normally into."

"Who do you normally date?" I asked.

"Assholes, mostly," said Heather. "Athletes and stuff.

I kind of picked Tim to like at random at first, back in, like, eighth grade, but he's such a great guy that I just never got over the crush, even if he is kind of a dork."

"He'd have to be a great guy to put up with Emma," I said. This was sort of true. Being in love with someone who didn't always process information rationally, like Emma, had to be hard.

"I know!" said Heather. "I guess he thinks that he can't do any better because he's sort of a geek, huh?"

"Maybe," I said.

I almost felt bad for Heather, honestly. She wasn't a villain or anything, other than calling Emma a manatee and starting a rumor about Tim, both of which were really uncool. But I knew what a crush felt like, and she was about to be badly let down.

I guess that's just the way it goes sometimes.

After all, she seemed to think she was entitled to go out with Tim just because she was pretty. It takes more than that to deserve someone's love.

I still felt bad for her, in a way, but hopefully this would get her over Tim and let her move on to someone who brought out the best in her.

When we made it to the record store I told Heather to go hide out by the T-shirts until I gave her a signal. While we waited for Emma and Tim, I flipped my way through the Beatles albums, pausing to consider picking up a copy of *Abbey Road* because Emma had said it was proof that there was magic in the world. I thought

I recognized one or two of the song titles on the back, but I wasn't certain. I had a lot of catching up to do, music-wise.

But I was also broke.

Every couple of seconds, I glanced out the door, down the main walkway to the theater on the other end. I hoped Lisa wouldn't come bursting out until I finished up with this quest of my own. If she came storming out looking upset, I'd have to leave the store behind and go to her. I was pretty sure Emma could still get away from Heather again if she had to, but then my quest to get the two of them face-to-face would have to be a quest for another day.

I tried to plan what the heck I was going to say when I saw Lisa, anyway. If she didn't come bounding out looking distraught and in need of comfort, maybe I could say something funny and make her laugh. Then I'd say a line from that one Beach Boys song Uncle Jesse sang on the wedding episode and just watch her heart melt.

It seemed like a pretty smooth way to do things, if I had the guts and a whole lot of luck and maybe some sort of divine help.

Come on, St. Merle the Naked, I thought. *I'm counting on you now.*

Meanwhile, while all this crap was running through my brain, Heather was still flipping through T-shirts. She didn't seem too nervous at all, but she also wasn't being entirely patient. After a few minutes, she turned to me and said "Well?"

"Just hang on," I said. "They're coming."

After ten minutes, just like we agreed, Emma and Tim walked into the store.

"Did you lose her?" asked Emma.

"No," I said. "I think you need to talk to her. Now, Heather!"

I ran around behind Emma and Tim to block the door.

Emma turned and looked at me with a horrified expression as Heather turned from the T-shirts to face them. Emma grabbed Tim by the arm and started to run, but I blocked her.

"You need to get this over with, Emma," I said.

"How could you?" Emma asked me, starting to hyperventilate. "How could you?"

"Watch what happens," I said. "This is a holy quest."

"Tim!" said Heather. "I have to talk to you. In private."

"You can talk to me here," said Tim, who sounded confused.

"I was wondering if you wanted to go out sometime, Tim," said Heather. "With me."

Emma just about collapsed against me.

I looked at Heather—she had dressed for this occasion. Her boobs were almost popping right out of her shirt.

Tim looked shocked.

"Huh?" he asked.

"I'm serious," said Heather. "This bitch has been trying to keep me from you, but she can't run anymore. I've had, like, the biggest crush on you since middle school. You want to go see a movie? Or go for a drive? Or go to my place? My parents aren't there. We can do anything we want."

Emma started to say something, but Heather interrupted.

"Don't you dare say a word this time, Wolf," she said. "I've had enough of your fat ass!"

Emma looked like she had been punched.

Heather turned back to Tim, who looked too shocked to say anything. "Those calls from the debt collector have been from me. I've been trying to call you forever," she told him. "The manatee messed with your phone. Your computer too, probably. You never got my emails, did you?"

Tim shook his head.

"Go ahead, Tim," Emma muttered. "I don't blame you. Go with her. You can probably get laid tonight."

I could almost see the wheels in Tim's head turning as he figured out the whole thing. And then he smiled.

"Can I ask you something?" he asked Heather.

Heather nodded.

"Are you Bluish?" asked Tim.

"What?" asked Heather.

"Sorry, but it's against my religion to date girls who aren't Bluish."

I couldn't help but say, "You don't look Bluish" to Heather.

I don't know who looked more shocked—Emma or Heather. Neither one could believe Tim was saying no. Emma was sobbing.

"She's serious, Tim," Emma whimpered. "You don't have to scare her away. You can go be with her. I won't blame you."

Tim turned to Emma and sort of held her enough to keep her from collapsing. "Did you really make it look like she was a debt collector calling?"

"Yeah." Emma nodded. "And all of her emails get sorted into your trash folder automatically."

"You're totally going to Nebraska," he said.

She nodded again, and he sort of chuckled.

"Don't worry," he said. "I'll go there with you."

It took her a second to register what he'd said.

"For real?" She was barely whispering.

"Yeah," said Tim. "I swear to Bob. But Bluists never die."

And he kissed her on the mouth. Emma slowly went from looking shocked to leaning into the kiss. Well, standing upright into it, and *then* leaning into it.

They weren't in a graveyard, but a record store would do.

Heather looked at me. "How can they not die?"

"None of them have yet," I said.

When Tim finally came up for air, Emma looked dazed.

238

"Holy shit," she said.

Tim was right. Anything can happen on a night when you cross off the last three goals on a holy quest checklist.

Suddenly, there was a big flash of light. For a split second, I thought it was an actual Spark of Blue, but then all of the lights except for the emergency lights next to the fire alarms turned off.

The storm had knocked the power out. People began to groan.

"Run, Debbie," said Tim. "People are going to be leaving the theater. Go get her!"

In the dark, I couldn't see the look on his face, or on Emma's or Heather's. And I didn't stick around to look.

I ran like a bat out of Nebraska.

* Twenty-one *

I raced through the mall at top speed. The dim beams of the emergency lights lit my way back to the theater, where the first waves of people had already started walking out into the lobby. Every few seconds there was a flash of light coming through the glass doors that opened to the parking lot. Lightning.

I strained my eyes and spotted Lisa, walking hand in hand with Norman out of the theater, past the box office. Seeing them touching hurt—especially now that I knew she was probably planning to let him touch a lot more than her hands—but at least they were *there*, not just sitting in the now-empty theater, taking advantage of the dark.

My knees were shaking. My shirt was damp against my skin and still had snot and yogurt stains on it. The sweater I had on over it smelled like incense and mold. My forehead was wet, and I wasn't sure if it was because my hair was still wet from the rain, or if it was just sweat. Coming out to Lisa wasn't such a huge deal, really, but saying how I felt about her was something else entirely.

"Lisa!" I shouted.

She turned toward me and looked surprised for a second, then smiled that beautiful smile I'd been living to see for the last five years.

"Can you come here for a second, please?" I asked.

She let go of Norman's hand, told him she'd be right back, and walked over to me. Norman gave me a weird look, but I ignored him and led Lisa away from the crowd and over to the wall.

And for one second, the only thing I could think of was the *Full House* episode where Joey takes Stephanie to the dentist, holds a mirror up to her mouth, and tells her that her uvula is her Courage Hangy-Ball. The part of her body that gave her courage.

I gulped as Lisa got closer to me. But not because I was nervous. I was making sure my Courage Hangy-Ball was still there.

"I got your message," she said. "Your keys were in my front seat. I was going to call you after the movie."

She pulled them from her purse and handed them to me.

"Thanks," I said. "You know what a klutz I am!"

"Totally," she said.

I almost started counting to twenty-five, but then I stopped myself. There was no time, and no reason to keep covering my thoughts.

"Listen," I said. "I need to talk with you."

"What's up?" Lisa asked. "Are you okay? Angela said you were really upset about something earlier."

I stared at her for a second and gulped again. I felt like I should open with a joke or something, but I couldn't think of one.

"Well, I have a confession to make," I said.

"Can it wait til tomorrow?" she asked. "This kind of seems like a weird place for something like that, don't you think?"

"No," I said, shaking my head. "It has to be now. Because you're going to find out pretty soon anyway. And I want you to hear it from me, not, like, from Norman."

I took a deep breath. I'd always sort of hoped that one day she'd make the first move. But that was incredibly stupid of me.

And now I had to do it in public. I doubted anyone was actually looking, but I felt like everyone in the mall was. I couldn't remember any of the song from Uncle Jesse's wedding anymore. I just forced myself to open my mouth.

"I like girls," I said, very softly. I looked down at the floor, afraid to see the look on her face. "You, mostly."

And then, just as I said that, there was this lightning

flash. It might have been my imagination, but I could have sworn it was blue, not white or yellow like most lightning.

In that moment, it occurred to me that I didn't want to go to ACTs again.

And I didn't want to miss out on finding weird places to put stolen Neighborhood Watch signs. Or on planting pressed hams at the governor's mansion. I'd even press one myself, if the windows were low enough to the ground.

In a weird way, I *almost* wanted her to turn me down.

This hit me in a split second, and I think I had the fastest panic attack in history in the time it took to take one sharp breath. I was panicking that she might get freaked out, *and* afraid that she might say she loved me, too.

But she didn't do either of those.

She acted like I'd told her I liked ice cream.

"I know you do," she said.

My breath went back to normal, and I felt *something* going on inside me, but I couldn't tell whether I was blushing, or wetting myself, or about to barf, or what. It was just … something. Too much at once.

I looked back up at her. She didn't look shocked or appalled at all. "What?" I asked.

"I've known that since, like, seventh grade."

"What?" I said again.

"I mean, honestly," said Lisa with a laugh. "I change into my swimsuit behind a towel around you!"

"What?" I said, yet again. It's like every other word had been punched out of my brain.

"And I can never talk about sex with you, because I'm afraid it would be, like, teasing you or something."

I took a second to let my vocabulary pick itself off the floor and crawl back into me. It came back slowly, a couple of words at a time.

"Uh, sorry," I said finally.

"It's okay," she said. "We had to have this talk sooner or later! But you like guys too, right?"

I kind of shrugged and stood there looking like a damp idiot.

"Norman told me you and Aaron really hit it off today. Want me to fix it up?"

I couldn't think of what to say. I just said, "Uh … yeah."

Lisa reached over and hugged me. "It's going to be okay," she said.

Norman made his way up to us and put his arm around Lisa's waist, but I was too dazed to react very much.

"Is something wrong?" he asked.

"No," said Lisa, moving up against him. "Nothing's wrong. Right, Deb?"

"Uh … right," I said.

"Don't worry, honey. We'll fix you up with Aaron this week, and he'll make you'll forget all about … the other person you like."

I nodded a bit and tried to get my eyes to focus

again. For a second I thought I heard a train coming right through the mall to run me over, but it was just a roll of thunder.

How much of Lisa's uptightness all those years had been an act, just for my sake? Maybe she really was like that when she was eleven, and over the years she'd gotten more open-minded on premarital sex and stuff, but still acted like she wasn't so I wouldn't get all gay on her.

That's what I *should* have been thinking. But I wasn't. My brain was so mixed up that all I could think about at the moment was that Lisa was right: Norman really did dress like he was going fishing for trout.

"We'll talk tomorrow, okay?" said Lisa.

I nodded.

The instant she turned around, the lights in the mall came back on.

The tinny speakers in the ceiling buzzed, then started playing a Beach Boys song—"Help Me, Rhonda."

My knees got so weak that I had to sit down on the ground. My whole body shook. But then there was this huge crash of thunder and I just felt numb, even though I had just been rejected in front of a live studio audience. I thought I was crying, but I couldn't tell.

"Debbie!" someone called.

It was Emma. She and Tim ran up to me.

"What happened?" Tim said.

I looked up at them, hovering above me like I was a patient on a gurney. I didn't feel like the juice was coming out of my heart anymore. I felt like I was sort of floating outside of myself.

"She said she knew I liked her the whole time," I said. "And then she said she'd hook me up with Aaron Riley and I'd forget all about her. Then they just left."

"How rude," said Emma.

And that's when I started to giggle. I don't know if Emma had intended to use the ultimate *Full House* catch-phrase, but she had. And at just the right time.

I looked up to see Lisa and Norman's backs as they left the building. Something about the picture of the two of them eating plain oatmeal together when Norman woke up early for a trout-fishing adventure suddenly struck me as incredibly funny. My giggles turned to actual laughs.

I was definitely crying now, but I was laughing, too.

"You okay?" asked Tim.

"She's laughing," said Emma. "Blue is mysterious."

I was back inside myself. I had floated out just far enough to find the humor in the situation, and come back.

Then I forgot about myself for a second and noticed that Emma and Tim were holding hands.

"See?" I asked. "He didn't ditch you!"

"Of course I didn't," said Tim. "Thanks, Debbie."

"It was a holy quest," I said. "Matter of the heart. Commandment number one."

"I'm still scared," Emma said. "I still feel like you'd dump me as soon as you meet someone less psychotic."

"Never gonna happen," said Tim.

"I'm really high maintenance."

"I am, too. And we're good at maintaining each other."

Twin high-maintenance machines.

"Are you guys official now?" I asked.

"We'll see," said Emma. "We haven't really had time to talk about it."

I scanned around the mall to see if Heather was coming up behind us or something. There was no sign of her.

"What happened to Quinn?" I asked.

"She swore she'd get revenge," said Emma. "She actually raised a fist and said, 'He will be mine!'"

I laughed.

"She can dream on," said Tim.

"She'll find someone who compliments her better," I said. "That was a matter of the heart, too. Letting her find out that she needs to get over her crush."

For a second, we all just stood there—or sat there, in my case. I sat there and laughed, even though I was also crying, and thought about how funny it was to be, well ... to be anything, really. Blue, or whatever it was that ran the universe, definitely had a weird sense of humor.

"Are you sure you're okay?" Emma asked. "After the whole thing with Lisa?"

"Actually," I said, "I'm almost relieved. But I think I need a quick favor."

"Sure," said Emma.

I hoisted myself up. "Follow me for a second."

I grabbed her by her free hand and took her all the way back to the record store. Tim followed.

There was something I had to do.

In the store, I looked along the wall of CDs that were hooked up to pairs of headphones, and found a pair connected to something called *Jazz for a Relaxing Afternoon*. I turned it on, put the volume as high as it would go, and set the headphones on the stand so that we could hear the music playing faintly out of them.

"Okay," I said. "Give me a talk."

"A talk?" asked Emma.

"This is how *Full House* episodes always end," I said. "Someone gives someone else a talk, there's soft music in the background, and then they all hug and everything's okay. I put the music on, now give me the talk, and we'll hug."

"What should I talk about?" asked Emma.

"Whatever," I said. "Just teach me a valuable lesson."

I sat down on the floor and looked up at her.

Emma, for once, looked sort of like she was at a loss for words.

"Ummm, you know, Debbie," she said. "John Lennon said that life is what happens while you're busy making other plans. But some things don't really work out the way you planned for them to. And that's life."

"Keep going," I said. "Something about being yourself."

"You see, Debbie," she said, sounding more confident and using something like a "parent" voice, "you shouldn't try to change yourself just to get someone to like you. If a person doesn't like you for who you are, they aren't worth liking. When you find the right girl, it will be that much more special."

"I know," I said. "I understand."

"So, are you going to be okay?" she asked.

I nodded and stood back up.

"Now we hug," I said. "And Tim, you go 'Awwww.'"

Emma opened up her arms and we hugged in the middle of the aisle, while soft music played and the Apostle Tim went "Awwww."

Then Tim joined in on the hug, so we were all having one big group hug and saying "Awwww."

It was the end of a very special multi-part episode of *The Wonderful World of Lisa*. The conclusion of a plot line the writers had dragged out for five years.

During those five years, I didn't really know how to be myself. I'd spent so much time trying to be the person I thought would have the best chance with Lisa that I had no clear idea who "myself" was anymore.

It was like in the song. Only God knew who I'd be without Lisa. Or maybe Blue only knew. Or maybe only some naked angel racing above my head on a tricycle of fire knew.

Anyway, *I* didn't know.

But I was ready to find out.

✴ Twenty-two ✴

So, Blue didn't answer my prayer when I asked to be brought together with Lisa. Neither did any of the other deities I'd dropped a line to. Maybe they were all offended that I wasn't being exclusive with them.

Or, actually, maybe one of them *had* answered me. The answer just happened to be "no."

There's an old Garth Brooks song Lisa used to like—and that I always thought was pretty good, myself—about how sometimes God's greatest gifts are unanswered prayers.

The way I'd been clinging to her, and trying to be like her, was like trying to sell my soul to get into heaven.

After leaving the mall, Tim, Emma, and I turned in enough empty pop cans at the nearest Hy-Vee to buy the gas to get us home, then went over to my house to switch to my car. From there, we headed down to Urbandale to the house where Angela was babysitting and told her the whole story of the night.

It turned out that Angela's first kiss was in a graveyard, too—the little one on Meredith Street. I didn't ask what the hell she was doing in that one, which didn't have any haunted houses or graves that were supposed to be enchanted or anything, in the first place. I just knew—she and some guy must have been drawn there by the same weird energy that made people declare it consecrated ground to start with.

Once it began to sink in that it was really over between Lisa and me, I started getting a little depressed—regardless of anything else, I was still basically losing the girl who had been my best friend for years.

But it wasn't an "I'll never be happy again" depression, or even an "I need to move to Minneapolis and get away from all this" depression. It was the kind you get after you watch the brilliant series finale of your favorite TV show. Even though the last episode was done perfectly, it sucked to know there'd never be another one, unless they did a reunion show something years later. But the feeling would pass. There would be other shows. The show had gone downhill in the last couple of seasons, anyway. It was time for it to end before it got any worse and made me less interested in buying the Complete Series set, which would probably come in a neat box.

We hung around at the house until after midnight.

Tim and Emma held hands the whole time, and even dared to kiss a couple more times. They were approaching being a couple cautiously. Emma kept looking like she expected him to change his mind any second.

"This isn't a requirement," she told him. "There's no rule about Bluists having to date other Bluists."

"Well, I know that most modern Bluists date outside their faith," said Tim. "But I'm Orthodox."

And he kissed her again.

I got home after midnight (for the first time in my life) and collapsed into a dreamless sleep.

By the end of Saturday morning, I'd decided that I was officially joining the Church of Blue. Or, anyway, I'd decided to start pretending that I was a member of a pretend religion called Bluedaism.

I was going to miss seeing my mom looking uncomfortable but trying to act like she was cool with me going to ACTs. And I didn't agree with everything Emma had made up, like the idea that everyone has a single "Spark of Blue" inside them. Why just one? I'll bet everyone is full of a thousand different kinds of sparks.

But Bluedaism was a good thing to hold on to while I tried to figure the rest of the world out. It had worked out pretty well so far. And I was sure, now, that there was some sort of force in the universe that was capable of helping people create great works of art, of turning out the lights at exactly the right second, of putting the right music on the radio, and of delivering me from Aaron Riley.

I asked Emma how one goes about formally converting, and she said that, since it was a made-up religion, I could make up my own conversion ritual.

So three days later, on Monday, the first official day of spring break, Emma, Tim, and I were in my bathroom and my head was in the sink. I was dying a bright blue highlight into my hair.

If I'd told Lisa I was going to do that, she probably would have tried to talk me out of it.

But this wasn't her life, or her hair. It was mine.

"All right," said Emma. "I think it's all rinsed off. Now get in the shower, shampoo your hair, and keep rinsing til the water's clear, not blue. Then we'll get it dry."

I shooed Emma and Tim out the door, took my clothes off, and climbed into the shower. Every time I'd bathed or gotten wet or changed cloths or anything in the past couple of days, it had felt like another baptism. A washing away of what had been there before.

In a way, I had already been Bluish when I left the girls' room on Friday afternoon. Symbolically flushing myself down the toilet to start my new life had been a perfect idea for a Bluish ritual.

I just hoped my hair looked good for the new holy quest that night. We were going to start by putting up a Neighborhood Watch sign at the Wells Fargo headquarters, then see what other places we could find to put them.

When I felt like I'd shampooed enough, I stepped out, dried off, and got into my new clothes—a sun dress with blue splotches, which I hoped would match my new hair. The mirror was too fogged up for me to see how anything looked, but I shook my hair out, then wrapped a towel around it so it wouldn't drip on my dress and headed out into my bedroom.

Emma was playing *Abbey Road* on the stereo—I recognized it right away. Over the weekend, she'd given me crash courses in all the music she thought I should know about. Some of it I liked, some of it I didn't. But at least I felt like I could think about the songs out loud, instead of worrying that people would read my mind and know that I didn't believe in most of what the singer was singing, like I always did with Lisa's music. Hell, I could even say that I didn't like them out loud. The worst that ever happened was that Emma would insist it would grow on me.

"All right," she said. "Have a seat."

Emma turned my desk chair so it faced away from the mirror, and I sat down. She removed the towel from my head. Tim started working the blow dryer on me while Emma ran her fingers through my hair.

"How's it look?" I asked.

"Can't tell yet," said Emma. "Give it a few more minutes to dry out."

I wasn't over Lisa, by any means. You can't just forget

someone after five years when they've totally defined your life. Whenever I saw something funny, my first thought was still that I couldn't wait to tell Lisa about it. And when I thought about her and Norman kissing, or even doing more than that, it still made me feel a little bit sick to my stomach.

But I was into a new phase of my life.

No more *Wonderful World of Lisa*. No co-starring with anyone. I was going to be starring in the lead role on my own spin-off.

I even had an "appointment" with Moira to go to Java Joe's on Wednesday. I wasn't quite ready to call it a "date" yet; it seemed dangerous to let myself go ahead and start liking—I mean, like, *like* liking—Moira. The practical time traveling thing was cute, but I could imagine it getting old, and I had been sort of living in a bygone era long enough.

But all crushes are risky. I was lucky to have escaped my crush on Lisa alive.

I was pretty sure I'd never watch an episode of *Full House* again, but I didn't curse the day I'd seen it anymore. It may have given me weird ideas about love and romance, but it also taught me to be brave and stick by the people who needed me.

"Okay," said Emma, turning the blow dryer off. "Stand up and turn around."

I stood up from the chair and faced the mirror.

There I was. With a streak in my hair so dark it was

almost black, but if you looked at it just right, it really was a deep midnight blue. It matched the dress perfectly.

"Awesome," said Tim.

"You look gorgeous," said Emma. "We're going to have to keep you away from the bowling alley from now on. Ramona and her friends would be all over you!"

"I was thinking we'd start the holy quest tonight at the malt shop in Beaverdale, anyway," said Tim. "We can have some ice cream and brainstorm twenty goals for the new checklist before we go to Wells Fargo."

"Cool," said Emma. "We can stop at the governor's mansion on the way to see what security is like there. And cross that one off, if security's not too tight."

"You don't have to do it if you don't want to, Debbie," said Tim.

"I think I can manage it," I said, even though I wasn't totally sure.

I smiled at myself in the mirror. A whole new version of me.

I don't think there'll ever be a version of me that doesn't love Lisa, at least in some way or another. Even when I'm eighty, I'll want to know where she lives, what she's made of herself, whether she's happy. But the day before spring break, the thought of not being there *with* her at eighty would have made me feel like I wanted to die.

And now I knew I could move on. I wasn't dying without her.

I was busy being born.

About the Author

S. J. Adams is a high-ranking member of the staff that produces the Smart Aleck's Guide series. At headquarters, S. J.'s job includes everything from saving Adam Selzer (boss of the Smart Aleck staff) from ghosts to giving the interns their baths (and silencing the ones who discover the secret codes revealing the secret identity of the *real* author of Adam's books). You can find S. J. (pronounced "Sij") all over the Internet, starting at smartalecksguide.com.